THE

PI(E)

TRUCE

DAYA JAMES

Table of Contents

Diana and Carson's Playlist

I Can't Stand It - Harbour
Campus - Vampire Weekend
Real Estate - Adam Melchor
Diana - One Direction
Florida! - Taylor Swift ft. Florence + the Machine
All Falls Down - Lizzy McAlpine
Dirty Diana - Michael Jackson
Fearless (Taylor's Version) - Taylor Swift
Cherry Wine - Zachary Knowles
Almost (Sweet Music) - Hozier
Kiss Her You Fool - Kids that Fly
Stop - Anthony Ramos
Used to Me - Luke Chiang
Late Night Talking - Harry Styles
New Perspective - Noah Kahan
Honey - Coastal Club
Liz - Remi Wolf
De Selby (Part 1) - Hozier
House Song - Searows
Cherry Wine - Hozier
TubThumping - Chumbawamba
Like to Be You (feat. Julia Michaels) - Shawn Mendes
Malibu - Miley Cyrus
Meddle About - Chase Atlantic
The Scientist - Coldplay
Someone New - Hozier

Unkind – Taylor Bradshaw

Prologue – Not-So Sweet Revenge
Carson

Late July

Nothing screams summer like a good prank.

I stand by the unoccupied house, hiding with a lemon meringue pie at the ready for my best friend, Jake Parker, to show up. Earlier this morning, I woke up to a pie in the face thanks to him and figured it was time to return the favor.

So when he left for the gym in the morning, I took it upon myself to walk to the village and grab a frozen lemon meringue pie that I let thaw.

Given how hot it can get in July, and in Los Angeles of all places, it didn't take very long.

Every time I hear something move even slightly, I can't help but turn my head to see if that's Jake, but it always ends up being some neighbor passing by, taking out the trash or a car horn.

It's Thursday morning, for crying out loud. How are the streets so busy?

Jake and I arrived yesterday and two of our roommates—Adrian and Enzo—are supposed to be coming later this evening. There's much more for me to do, like settle into my room, but it can wait once I get even with Jake.

I check my watch, seeing the hour hand at one. How long does it take someone to work out? Jake is not even a gym rat.

The creaky fence alerts me and the sound of crunching dirt gets louder, breaking me out of my thoughts. Finally, he's here. Pie in hand and determination set, I lunge out of my hiding place and smack the pie square onto his face.

A gasp takes me by surprise, because of how high-pitched it was. As far as I know, we don't have any girls living in the house in front of us.

I realize that the footsteps I heard earlier do not belong to my best friend. The people—yes, I mean people—were actually two unfamiliar girls around my age. One of whom is now covered in lemon meringue pie from the neck up.

A short girl with long dark braids has one hand over her mouth and stands at a distance from me and her—I assume—friend. Her brown eyes are wide as we watch her friend wipe the filling from her eyes and mouth.

"Oh. My. Gosh." The girl covered in pie narrows her bright hazel-green eyes at me. "Are you fucking insane?!"

Holy cracked knuckles, she's got a set of lungs.

"Hey, what's with all the comm—oh shit!" Jake stops in his tracks and takes in the scene in front of him. His jaw drops slightly when he realizes what just happened.

I narrow my eyes at him. "You couldn't have come earlier?"

He shakes his head and walks around the girl, towards our house. "You dug this grave on your own, Carson! I'm staying out of this shit." *That son of a bitch.*

Clearly, I've never put myself in a situation like this before—thrown pie at an unsuspecting cute girl and gotten yelled at by said girl—so I'm a little lost for words at the moment. All that falls out of my mouth is, "I swear that was an accident."

But the brunette standing in front of me is full of more words than a dictionary. "Yeah, and I *accidentally* chose to live in front of an overgrown child. Totally my fucking mistake."

She turns on her heels and storms off. Her friend doesn't follow behind, instead choosing to stay in her spot. "You definitely made an impression on her."

I let out a breath and run one hand through my brown hair. "You think she'll forget?"

She scoffs. "Never. Diana doesn't forget things like that. I'm just glad it didn't hit me."

Ah, so the spitfire has a name. I arch a brow at the girl in braids. "You wouldn't want pie in the morning?"

"I wouldn't want pie at all," she emphasizes before holding out her hand to me. "I'm Lucia, by the way. We just started moving our stuff in so she's a little tight-wounded. Don't mind her."

I grab her hand and shake it. For a girl so small, she's got a tight grip. "Well, I hope she doesn't hold it over me for the next twelve months." I glance at the trail leading to the gate, where drops of pie filling lead like footsteps, getting smaller and smaller.

Lucia laughs. "With Diana, anything's possible."

"Even forgiveness?"

She nods. "That's possible. Maybe don't bring a pie with you the next time you speak with her."

1

What the Heck?

Diana

October

I can sense doomsday coming as my now-graded calculus midterm is placed on my desk, face-down.

Mathematics was never my strong suit—especially calculus. Numbers and letters? I don't care what anyone in my major of classical studies says—the Sumerians were high as fuck back then.

Same with Newton. Fuck that guy.

The test is face down on my desk and my table mate Lucia is staring down at her paper, frown lines creasing her brows. That's not a good sign. She's a psychology major but chose to take this class with me because both of us were in dire need of fulfilling our general math credits to graduate.

Neither of us needs it for our respective careers but apparently, the private prissy school that is the University of Southern California requires it.

Lucia, however, is much better at math than I am; if she were to not do well on this particular exam, then there's not a doubt in my mind that I am utterly fucked.

I tried my best—I really did—but I guess there was no hope for me after all.

Closing my eyes, I slowly flipped my test over and creaked one eye open. In red ink, near the top of the paper where my name is written, is the number seventy circled messily.

Oof, a low C. That's not good. Let doomsday begin. I can smell the failure already.

"Lucia," I whisper. "What did you get?"

Her brown eyes trail over to me, panic lacing the dark irises. She shakes her head slightly, giving me the signal that I dreaded: she didn't do well, either.

I read over the markings my professor made on each question, my heart beating faster and faster with each incorrect answer. This was the midterm I'd been studying my ass off for weeks yet, unlike history and other humanities, numbers were never a breeze.

"Maybe the scores will be curved," Lucia whispers. "If everyone else did as bad as us, then that could end up being a B instead of a C." She taps a dark green fingernail on my test.

I swivel my head around the classroom, not as hopeful as my friend. Unlike most of my classical studies lectures, the size of this class is approximately twenty or thirty students, give or take. With every class, there's always that one kid who will ruin it. I scan the classroom at each person, wondering who it could be.

Who could play a contributing factor in my future?

I can't afford for my grade to go any lower than its current standing, which isn't great. My entire undergrad depends on this.

"Okay, students," Professor Scott's booming voice brings us all to our attention. Though he may be in his sixties, with graying hair and what my mother would call "old man glasses" perched on top of his head, he still has that ability to silence an entire room of students who are just impatiently waiting to walk across that stage and be handed their diploma. "I hope you had enough time to review your scores. Put them away, as we'll be moving on to the next chapter."

Someone must have raised their hand because after reaching the wood podium, he calls out, "Yes, Bailey?"

I turn around to find the box-blond in a red crewneck with the school's logo, much like half of the class, seated at the very back. Bailey Emerson. I'm not familiar with her but my roommates attend a couple of the parties that her sorority hosts.

"Will our scores be curved this time around?"

Scott pinches his nose and sighs. From where I'm seated—the second to the first row—it's a very visible sigh. He was expecting someone to ask that. "I'm afraid not this time, Ms. Emerson."

"What was the highest score?" Bailey asks, in that nasally voice that drives me insane; even though I don't believe she's annoying, precisely. I just don't associate myself with her social circles.

Though I must admit, I am curious about the scores.

"A ninety-five," he answers. "It was the only A in this class so the rest of you better study harder for the next quiz. I won't go so easy."

My eyes widen and I swear I hear someone choking on air in surprise. A ninety-five? Only one righteous asshole with the brain of Einstein or Athena got an A on the midterm? Honestly, I'm a little scared for the rest of the semester if everyone else did so terribly.

Scott moves onto the lecture and I try my best to keep up. The thing with calculus is that the subject is so meticulous. One little slip-up and you could go downhill. The stakes are so much higher with math and science than with English and History. In the humanities, there are so many interpretations of stories and past events.

Math? There's only one answer. Everything else is wrong.

At least, that's how I see it.

When class is over, Lucia and I walk out of the classroom—where I find myself glaring at another guy who bumped into me—and out of the building, heading towards the Main Library before my shift begins. She also needs to start on another paper for one of her psychology classes.

"Hey, what are you doing tomorrow?" She asks while we look at the shelves for a particular book she asks.

I shrug. "Homework, work, and *Gilmore Girls*."

She chuckles. "You do that every day, though."

I nod. I don't need to argue otherwise—Lucia has been one of my best friends since we were both assigned roommates our first year in the dorms. Even now, we live off-campus with each other; along with two other girls and one guy because housing in South Central Los Angeles is crazy expensive.

"I'll order takeout this time," she assures me. "I still owe you for introducing those Croquetas to me. They were heavenly."

I grin. "No need. You showed me what real Ethiopian food is supposed to taste like." Lucia is technically an Eritrean-American to her core but because her culture isn't well known due to how fucked up it can be—her words, not mine—Ethiopian food is the closest we can get.

She pushes each book aside and reshuffles them. I groan internally, knowing that I'm the one who will have to arrange them. Why can't people have enough human decency to just place their book exactly where it's supposed to go? It not only drives me crazy but the head librarian has the absolute worst case of OCD.

If she suffers, then so does everyone else.

A phone ringing breaks through the silence of the library. The Main Library is usually pretty quiet, especially on Fridays, when everyone is getting ready for the weekend, doing who the hell knows what.

Lucia checks her phone and her dark eyes widen. "You will not believe what Bailey just sent me, D."

I raise a brow, busying myself with reorganizing the books. "What now?"

"She just found out who got the A."

My hands freeze over an old book I don't bother reading the spine of. "So?"

"Aren't you curious to know? Isn't that little voice in your head telling you to prod me for details?"

Honestly? Yes. I wanna know the name of the son of a bitch (or just, bitch) who messed with everyone else's grade.

I give in to my curiosity and wait for Lucia to show me the screen so I can go find the person responsible.

My jaw drops in horror. "No."

2

Give Me A Break

Carson

"Hey, *compa*," my housemate, Enzo greets me as I close the door behind me and slip my sneakers off. The most important rule in this house is to always slip my shoes off the moment I walk through this door. I don't understand why but it's the only rule that's been enforced in the three months we've been living here.

I grunt as I drop my bag onto the ground right in front of the couch and fall onto it, stomachside down. After the week I've been having, I'm fucking beat. The only bright light has been earning back my calculus midterm, which I had extremely low hopes about.

"One of those days?" He snorts, munching on something.

My groan is muffled through the couch cushions. Three more semesters of this and I'll be done with undergrad. That gap year is out of my reach but I can feel it inching closer.

And closer.

And closer.

I flip myself over onto my back, looking up at the light gray ceiling, and breathe in. "Thank fucking God it's Friday."

He rounds the kitchen counter and looks down at me. "Truer words have never been said." Enzo continues munching on something. I sit up on the couch and observe the bag of mini M&Ms on his left hand.

"Bro, are those my M&Ms?" I ask.

Enzo shrugs. "So?"

My jaw drops, slightly befuddled. "How did you find them?"

"Ryder, you suck at hiding your shit. I didn't do a hint of searching to find them."

I narrow my eyes on my best friend. If I suck at hiding my stuff, then Enzo Rivera sucks at lying about stuff. Sensing bullshit has always been a talent of mine, but with Enzo, I don't need to try.

"Okay," he relents. "I was looking for my projector in your room and just found them. I didn't search for them, specifically."

"Why didn't you ask the others?" I'm talking about our other three roommates. The loudest people I know—at least, in comparison to me and Enzo.

He gestures to the living room. "Do you see or hear them right now? Mason's working, Adrian's on set, and I think Jake is with his girlfriend or with his ex-frat brothers—that I'm not sure about."

"How are they still together, again?" I wonder aloud.

"Beats me, dude. Bailey must give some good head if Parker can deal with her nasal voice yapping in his ear twenty-four seven."

I fake-gag. "Dude, I did not need to hear that about my cousin, of all people." I hold my hand out for the M&Ms and Enzo pours a few into my hand. Holding back an eye roll, I take the bag with my free hand. "Next time, ask before you steal."

"Like you know how to share," he scoffs.

"You've met my sister, Enzo. I have no choice *but* to share." I pop the other chocolates in my mouth and munch while listening to the silence. My sister always says that for someone to be considered good company, you need to feel comfortable in their silence. Enzo is one of the few people I've found that with, along with the rest of my roommates.

"Did you find it?" I twist the bag of chocolate to seal it shut. "The projector?"

He shakes his head. "I'll ask Ronnie about it."

Now that has piqued my curiosity. Ronnie is one of our neighbors, in the house in front of us. Yeah, it's a weird arrangement because we get the backyard (or front yard, in our case) while they have the driveway.

I'm not complaining about the arrangement, since I hardly interact with them except for the occasional party that most of our neighbors attend.

Jake and I are curious as to whether or not Enzo and Ronnie have hooked up yet. I mean, it's only a matter of time because the tension between them is so thick that you'd need a fucking chainsaw to cut it.

"Which reminds me." Enzo walks into his room. A few minutes later, he comes out holding a bright orange spiral notebook. "Are you headed to the Main Library this evening?"

I nod. There's the matter of finishing the final touches on a group project due Monday for my human anatomy class. "Why?"

He holds out a bright red notebook to me. "Can you give this to Diana while you're there? Please?"

This is the third time I groan out loud. Not out of being tired but because I would have to interact with a girl who can't stand me *or* my guts.

The fall semester has resulted in me sharing my pre-calculus class with Lucia Abraham and Diana Blanco, who also live in the driveway house, as I have so named it. Imagine having to sit right behind them for two and a half months. Lucia has no problem with me, and I am with her. Diana on the other hand...

Let's just say that a girl walking into a prank warzone is not the best first meeting two neighbors could have. Ever. Especially when there's pie involved. She still holds that over me every time I'm around her.

Luckily, our only shared class is two days a week and she's never at the parties I attend. It's not like I have anything against her—if it wasn't for the pie incident, I would've attempted to ask her out a couple of times—but she's too stubborn to make conversation with me.

"Do I need to?"

"I will pay for coffee the next time we run out," he offers.

"Like you already do that," I remind him. "Why can't you do it, again?"

"I have to get ready for my closing shift and she needs it tonight. What do I need to do to convince you?"

Maybe create a time machine so that the pie incident didn't happen? That sure as hell would be nice.

"Are you hesitant because of the pie incident?" Enzo asks. "She still doesn't forgive you for that?"

I shrug. "Every time I see her in class, she's always giving me the stink-eye."

He winces. "Ouch."

I nod in agreement. I wouldn't wish the Diana Blanco stink-eye on anyone, not even my worst enemy—which in this case, is her. If that girl knew how scary she looked, especially with those burning hazel-green eyes of hers, I bet standing ten feet away would be her first reaction.

"So, throw a stink-eye back at her."

"Dude," I sigh. "I'll find another way."

"Oh, yeah. You've got a severe case of hate phobia." He rolls his eyes. "How could I forget?"

I flip my middle finger at Enzo, who just laughs it off. Hate-phobia makes no sense, whatsoever. Sure, I try my best to bring people peace and stay out of drama when possible but that doesn't mean that I can't stand the thought of people hating me.

Right?

"Ugh, fine," I give in. "But the next coffee I get from you better be free. And large."

"Deal," he says without a beat of hesitation. "Oh, didn't you get your midterm score?"

"Yes, Dad," I mutter, rolling my eyes. Enzo is the parent of our friend group if it's not obvious enough.

"So?"

I shoot him a look. "How do *you* think I did?"

He grins. "Knowing that you like to downplay how smart you are, I'd say pretty damn good."

Unfortunately for me, my best friend's not wrong. When Professor Scott announced the highest score in the midterm, I nearly choked on my breath. That couldn't have been possible whatsoever but after talking to him when the lecture ended, there was no denying it any longer.

Especially when sharing a class with my cousin Bailey, who didn't do as well on the test as I thought she would. She asked me countless questions after the exam and how I managed to score as high as I did.

I'm supposedly not as terrible as I thought. It only took countless hours of studying and though I would take biology over calculus any day of the fucking week, math was never much of a problem for me.

Though there's at least one person who just might have a problem *with* me.

3

Not Buying It
Diana

To anyone who wonders what it's like to work at a library, it's much better than being a barista. Why I never applied to work at a library during my high school years, I will never understand Sixteen-year-old me would have preferred to study during my breaks in the quiet instead of staying at home and helping my father with the basics.

When I'm not working, I still find myself in the Main Library, studying and working on my class papers. Sometimes, I watch a movie or an episode of *Gilmore Girls* but not as often as I'd like.

I'm sitting at the front desk of the library at the moment, where I am most of my shifts. It's been a couple hours since Lucia left and though I may have a neutral expression displayed on my face, I'm just about annoyed. Of all the people to have passed the midterm, why the fuck did it have to be him?

Carson fucking Ryder of all people (I don't even care to know his middle name). First, he purposely throws a lemon meringue pie in my face and now my math grade is possibly in jeopardy because of him? There isn't a Greek god of fucking with college students' lives but I know that everyone on Mount Olympus is laughing from up above.

Actually, I think that title belongs to Zeus. He's my least favorite out of all the Greek gods I've learned about over the years. If we were in ancient Greece instead of the modern world, Carson would be Zeus, and I'm the girl he's always messing with.

It's because of that *hijo de puta* I can't look at lemon meringue pie the same anymore.

"I need a study room," a deep voice says. I'm not looking straight ahead but mostly observing the computer screen in front of me. The screen just shows a fill-in-the-blank spot for all the study rooms.

"Can I see your ID?" I hold out my hand for the ID card and as soon as the cold card is placed in the palm of my hand, my eyes wander to the picture.

In an instant, I look away from the computer and scowl at the blue-eyed boy in front of me. "You."

Speak of the devil. Again, the gods are seriously fucking with my life because it's as if the boy was just poofed into thin air right in front of my damn face.

"Me," he taunts. "I need my ID back now."

I input his ID into the system and hand it back to him without sparing another glance at his bangs. See, it's already difficult enough to tolerate his presence in class and the house behind mine. Now my place of work? I take a deep breath, thinking on the bright side: at least we're not in the same program.

When I find myself looking back at the front, Carson's still standing there. For some odd reason. I don't need him to stand there like an Adonis for shits and giggles. Some people have work to do.

Wait, why did my mind go there? Adonis? I can describe Carson Ryder with a lot of adjectives—anything but Adonis, which is high praise from me. Praise that he doesn't deserve.

"What do you need?"

He frowns. "Aren't you supposed to tell me what room to go to?"

Oh, I almost forgot about that. My cheeks heat up slightly and I murmur, "Room 210. You know the drill." I hand him the key to the study room and he still hasn't moved. "Hit anyone with pies, lately?"

He smirks, no doubt unfazed by my question. "Only those who deserved it." Instead of turning away, he stuffs the key into the pocket of his denim jacket and reaches into his book bag to pull out a familiar-looking notebook.

Wait, that's mine.

"What are you doing with that?" I ask warily.

He holds it out to me. "Enzo told me to drop this off since he can't." His roommate and I share a class and since he's behind on the material, I volunteered my notebook so he could look over the notes. Or, in Enzo's case, take photos of them.

I hesitantly take it from his grasp, and in that brief interaction, the tips of my fingers brush his knuckles. On any other day, I wouldn't think anything into it.

Not today, apparently. His fingers are smooth, almost rich. It might be the weirdest thought to cross my mind in my junior year of college but that's honestly the best I can describe it. Honestly, nothing's hotter to me than a guy who knows how to take care of himself and not depend on anyone else.

"Something on your mind, Dirty Diana?"

I narrow my eyes at him. "Do *not* call me that." Ever again. Just...no. As much as I love my name, I don't like being compared to a Michael Jackson song that's about a creepy stalker. Carson doesn't have to remind me of the comparison every time I see him. Like before class, when he borrows something from my house.

Basically every fucking time he sees me.

I'm not even named after the song—though my mother used to love it—but whether or not he has decent intentions I still can't stand the nickname.

"Come on," he teases. "It's iconic."

"It's unoriginal, that's for sure," I mutter, rolling my eyes.

"Okay, maybe Sassy Diana is a better fit for you."

"That's even worse!"

"Well, then. What do you want me to call you?" He raises a challenging brow.

I sigh, my bangs lifting slightly. "Just Diana is fine." If it can get him to leave me alone and back to work. Or watching *Gilmore Girls* since it's pretty dead in here.

Carson tilts his head slightly, his chestnut-colored hair following the movements. I can't help but allow my eyes to follow it. How is it that someone who can get under my skin with ease could be blessed with such good hair? That's just unfair.

"Alright then, *Just Diana*, it is." He winks before walking off and it takes about half of my energy to restrain myself from lifting my middle finger at his retreating figure. I like nicknames as much as the next guy does—the only exception is when the next guy sucks at giving them out.

Carson knows how to pick at every bone in my body. Yet, somehow, I still let him.

"Who was that hottie?" A deep voice murmurs behind me.

I sigh. "No one important, Roman."

My coworker Roman sits his tall frame into the seat next to me. I'm not considerably short but anyone who stands near Roman Gregg would dwarf in comparison. We don't get scheduled together often but when it happens, he's a fun guy to be around.

"No one important, huh?" He wiggles his eyebrows as he enunciates each word. "Didn't seem like that by the way he was flirting with you."

I scoff, switching from one Microsoft tab to the other on the PC. "Flirting? That's hilarious, Roman."

"I'm serious," he insists. "It's plain as day."

"Okay, so what if he was flirting?" I ask, choosing to entertain Roman's factually incorrect theory as I take a sip from my water bottle.

"Easy. I'd reciprocate. Hit that faster than a lightning bolt strikes, hun."

The words cause me to choke on my water. "Roman!"

He shrugs. "I really would. Did you see him, D? He's like Jeremiah Fisher but more muscular and definitely straighter than an arrow."

"I saw him, alright," I mumble as I wipe the spilled water from my chin. Carson basically lives to irk me every waking moment. Though I can't lie about one thing—he is, to my annoyance, conventionally attractive. Hell, I even saw a couple of girls shooting me dirty looks when he was over there, but I don't think much of it. I take personality over looks like any girl with common sense.

"Besides, you're pretty, too. You got this whole Ana-De Armas-meets-Rory-Gilmore vibe going for you."

Coming from Roman, that's a compliment.

"Thanks," I tell him. "But there's no way in hell I'm getting with the bane of my existence."

"Bane of existence?" He stares at me with confusion in his eyes. "Wait, is this the same guy who threw a pie in your face?"

I nod curtly.

"So, we're supposed to hate him? And his cheekbones? D, you are not making this easy on me."

I nod again, crossing my arms. "It's bad enough that he lives in the house behind mine *and* that we share a class this semester. I don't need him coming to my place of work just to bother me."

"Maybe," Roman says. "And this is only a suggestion, Diana. He's not here just to annoy you." Shrugging, he adds, "and lots of students come to Main to study."

"I'll believe it when I see it."

He lets out a heavy sigh before standing back up. "Alright. But don't come to me when you find out that I'm right. Because I always am."

I roll my eyes as he goes back to the storage room. His words still ring in my head.

He's not here just to annoy you.

Really? Is that possible?

I shake my head. Not with Carson Ryder, it isn't.

4

I Have an Idea

Carson

It's pretty late when I get back to the house, which is as crowded as it can get with five guys in varying programs living under one roof.

Especially when three of them are squished on one bed, watching something on a laptop. Wow, that looks uncomfortable.

Since Enzo's still working, I'm left with the rest of my roommates. First, there's Adrian, who has this whole broody, mystery vibe on the outside. In reality, he's the biggest film geek I know.

Jake is squished in the middle, considering that he's the shortest after Enzo.

Finally, Mason. Aside from being the tallest of the five of us, he's also the smartest and pretty introverted. We don't see him around the house as much because of how dedicated he is to his studies.

Once I hear gunshots, I lean over Adrian's shoulder and glance at the movie they're watching. "What is this?"

Adrian is the first to respond. "*Die Hard*, duh. You know this, Carson."

"Yeah, I know." *Die Hard* is one of the best movies ever made. "Why are you watching it in the middle of October?"

"Because we can?" Mason asks, confusion lacing his face as he stares at the three of us like we're the Three Stooges. "It's our choice."

"Here we go," Jake mutters like he's about to hear my rant on the action film in front of us. "It's not a Christmas movie, Ryder. We've talked about this so many fucking times."

Of course, Jake knows what I'm going to say. "Does it take place during Christmas?"

He nods.

"Then I rest my case," I declare, throwing my hands up. "It's more appropriate to watch during the holidays."

"You are going to die on this hill, aren't you?" Adrian groans.

I raise both brows at him. Fuck yeah, I will. To me, it doesn't feel right to watch it any other time—except maybe in July, when the whole *Christmas in July* thing happens.

"I don't even know why I asked," he mutters to himself. "I've tried showing you much better movies but you always come back to this one but you hardly watch it."

"Miller, it's a matter of preference."

"Well, coming from me, your preference should expand to more than just Bruce Willis with a major superiority complex defeating Severus Snape."

"For your information," I argue. "I do watch other movies." Is that a lie? Kind of. Growing up, I was a little too busy to watch them. However, if someone had an extra ticket to the cinema or if Carly was watching a movie in the living room, then I would watch.

"Name one movie that doesn't belong to Disney or isn't in the *Die Hard* Franchise."

I lift a brow. "*Everything, Everywhere, All At Once.*"

He pinches the bridge of his nose. "That's on me for setting the bar too low." At my grin, Adrian narrows his eyes. "Oh don't act so smug, Ryder."

Shrugging helplessly, I hop onto the bed and squeeze myself next to Adrian. "Shall we continue?"

"Do you want us to start the movie over again?" Mason asks.

"No need," Jake answers for me. "At this rate, he can probably re-enact the entire film from start to finish."

I lean over to give Jake a shove, which has him tumbling over to Mason. The laptop tilts over on its side, resting on Mason's left knee. Just for one night, I let myself forget about my schoolwork. That's what Friday nights are made for—to relax. The rest you can worry about on Saturday and then relax again on Sunday.

Throughout the film, I start to realize why I don't watch movies with Adrian. He's a stand-up guy, I swear. However, his biggest weakness is the inability to hold back from making comments about production.

He is the only person I know who does this—aside from my sister, that is—and it's really fucking annoying.

"Adrian, if you make one more comment," Mason grumbles. At least he's not sitting next to the film critic.

3 . 1 4 1 5 9 2 6 5 3 5 9

"Hey, Carson," my cousin approaches me after our lecture. "Are you coming to tonight's party at my place?"

I shake my head as I shove my notebook into my backpack. "Sorry, Bales. I promised Carly I'd go to a screening of hers."

She rolls her blue eyes—ones very similar to mine. Despite being my cousin, she looks more like she could be my older sister, instead of being a year younger than I. "She's still in her film producer phase?"

I shrug. "That is what she's majoring in, after all."

"And she couldn't do that here instead of the rival campus?"

I don't remind Bailey about how my twin sister didn't get accepted into USC because it still stings. Not just for Carly. UCLA was her second-best option. It was also my first choice but I had been rejected.

"I gotta support my sister," I tell Bailey. Especially when my parents can't, or just choose not to. Like now.

"If this wasn't for Carly, I'd call you a people pleaser." She then taps her chin. "Wait, you still are."

I narrow my eyes. "No way."

"Cars, how are you at this school again?"

"Touché." I hate how she's right about that. My whole life has been built around not having a single person hate me. My family, friends, roommates—I would do just about anything. Obviously, I'm failing.

"You don't even want to stop by after?" She raises a brow. "I could introduce you to one of my sisters."

She's talking about her sorority sisters. Because Greek Row is *totally* the place to find a good hookup. "Maybe I'll stop by, but please don't set me up."

"Why not?" She tosses her blonde hair to her shoulder. "A lot of them want to meet you. Besides, if it wasn't for you, I wouldn't have found Jake."

"All I did was introduce you two," I point out. "You did the rest on your own." A lot of it. To this day, I haven't found a way to bleach the sound out of my ears without going deaf.

"I would beg to differ," my cousin huffs. "But I better see you there, even if it's for a minute."

"Don't count on it," I call after her as she saunters off towards one of her friends. I'm about to leave when a familiar voice causes my ears to perk up.

"I'm not doing it, Lucia."

"Diana," Lucia sighs in frustration. "You know what your counselor said!"

"I know but I can solve this myself."

Slowly, I turn my head to the source of the conversation. Sure enough, Lucia is standing over Diana, who is still seated in her chair. Her figure is almost bent over like a question mark,

Both girls have frustrated looks on their faces. Though Diana's is mixed with...defeat? That's odd.

"I don't want you to get kicked," Lucia says. "Just ask him or something."

"No," Diana responds harshly. "You know how I feel about—"

"Yes, I know but I don't care. And, frankly, you shouldn't either." Lucia moves her braids over to one shoulder. "Passing this class is far more important than holding a grudge."

I quickly look away, thinking she would have seen me watching them as she adjusted her hair.

Are they talking about me? About what?

"Sit on it, D," Lucia says with sincerity in her voice. "I would really hate for one stupid grade to fuck up your future."

And suddenly, a lightbulb turns on in my head.

As Lucia heads towards the door, I quickly grab her wrist, halting her. She looks up to meet my eyes and lifts a dark brow. "Why did you do that? A tap on the shoulder would have sufficed."

Whoops. "I need to ask you something."

She then lifts her other brow, intrigued. "Go on."

5

I'll Take The Pie

Diana

Just as I'm getting settled into the pull-out couch in the tiny-ass living room with my laptop, a can of cherry cola Olipop, and some leftover takeout from yesterday's Japanese late-night excursion, the fucking doorbell rings.

Who could be coming here this late? Everyone else is at a party—I didn't care to ask for the details, knowing damn well that I wouldn't be attending—and even the guys next door joined. My family back in Miami didn't plan a visit so...

I'm extremely confused.

The doorbell rings again.

Can't a girl watch *Harry Potter* and eat day-old sushi without interruptions? I want just one night to myself, where I can forget about all my responsibilities and the people in my life who drive me crazy. This is not the time for unwanted guests, even in my least respectable pajamas—my Hufflepuff set I bought at Universal Orlando with the logo so worn out it's almost gone.

The doorbell rings a third time and I groan out loud. Since it's just me, I hesitantly stand up and remove the blanket from my shoulders.

Maybe I need to be more social. I'm not shy, like my roommate Emma, but at least she chooses to go to parties and have fun. When I envision having fun, getting drunk, and grinding on sweaty frat boys is not the picture I paint in my head.

To each their own, I guess.

I don't even look into the peephole before opening the door and finding Carson Ryder, standing on my porch with a box in one hand. The box isn't even what catches my attention—nor is the black leather jacket that he dons, which shouldn't have made him look more like Logan Huntzberger than he already does—but the fact that he's even here has my gears spinning.

Narrowing my eyes at him, I decide to cut straight to the chase. "What are you doing here?" He could've used the back door but that's not at the forefront of my mind at the moment.

"Wow, what a way to greet your neighbor," he says with a hint of sarcasm, which vanishes as he takes in my pajamas. Again, not a pair I would feel comfortable wearing in front of anyone outside my family and roommates.

Carson does not fit in either category.

"What are you doing here?" I repeat, enunciating each word and drawing his attention from my slippers and back to my eyes. "There's no one else here."

"I know," he responds casually. "I came to see you."

What? He came here specifically to see me? That seems out of character for him—actually, him showing up without any of his buddies in the middle of a Friday night with a random box in hand is out of character for Carson.

I still don't say a word when Carson just lets himself in, stepping aside from me, my shoulder brushing his chest. Woah, that's a hard chest if I've ever felt one and he smells earthy, almost woodsy. Why is he making it so hard to be mad at him?

"You didn't go to the party?"

"What's with all the questions?" Carson sets the box on the countertop and takes a seat on the couch, next to the pile of blankets I had made for myself.

Please do not ruin it. If you were somewhat of a decent person not condemned to the Fields of Punishment, Carson whatever-your-middle-name-is Ryder, you would not ruin that perfect pile of blankets that took me longer to set up than I would like to admit.

Much to my delight, he dismisses the pile of blankets. "Well, if you're so curious, *Just Diana*, then no. I didn't go to the party."

Good. Not that I even cared in the first place. I'm just more concerned about my blankets.

"I'm not that curious," I argue.

"Admit it," he pesters. "You were wondering why I, of all people, would grace you with my presence."

I scowl. "More like why you're choosing to bother me instead of anyone else." That and what's inside of the box.

"Well," he begins. "I may or may not have overheard your little predicament from a friend of yours."

"What predicament?" I am extremely confused. And—to no one's surprise—annoyed. "Just cut to the chase, Ryder."

"Lucia told me about how you're struggling."

My eyes widen. Seriously? She went behind my back especially when I told her not to. "That blabbermouth," I mutter.

To preface, I'm attending university on a full scholarship—which I had worked four tirelessly long years of high school to achieve. It has always been that way as long as I could keep my grades up. That was never a problem for me until this semester when my calculus grade started falling faster than Hephaestus down Mount Olympus.

Greek mythology humor.

Because of the midterm, my calculus grade is inching closer and closer to a D, which is not something I've ever gotten before in my educational history. The only D I've ever received is the one in my name.

I'm already starting to hate that letter more and more with each passing minute.

"And," he continues. "I'm offering my services."

I tilt my head slightly. "Services?"

"To help you get your grade back up," he says, shrugging out of his jacket. "I thought that was obvious."

Carson is offering his help? Did hell freeze over? Is Zeus being faithful to Hera? What the ever-living fuck is going on here?

"What makes you think you're qualified?" Knowing him, he's probably never had to work so hard for anything a day in his life.

"For tutoring you in calculus?"

"Yes," I answer without hesitation.

Carson casually cracks each knuckle in his fingers. "Firstly, I'm the only one in our class who's *not* struggling to keep up with Scott's lectures."

This we already know, since he scored the highest in the midterm.

"Secondly," he continues, "you wouldn't be the first person I've tutored in math. So if you think I'm highly unqualified, let me be the first to say that you're wrong."

"So?" I shrug. "I'm not convinced."

His jaw slightly drops. "You'd rather fail a class than accept help from me?"

"Firstly, I can figure this whole thing out myself," I mention. "Without anyone else."

"Diana—"

"Plus," I cut him off. "I don't even like you." With tutors in the past, I barely knew them so there was nothing to go off of. Carson, however? I can barely go five minutes without the growing desire to smack him upside the head.

"At this point, you don't even have to like me," he says, frustration lacing those annoyingly bright blue eyes. "Just tolerate me for long enough to get your grade up."

Crossing my arms over my chest, I ask, "And how am I supposed to do that?"

"See, that's where this comes in." Carson gets up from the couch and reaches over to the countertop, where the box I've been eyeing sits. He opens it to reveal...

A pie.

More specifically, a rhubarb cherry pie. Like anyone with the last name Blanco, I am utterly weak for cherries of any and all variety. How...

"Lucia said something about you liking cherries," he explains, answering a question I didn't even speak aloud. Are his ears turning pink, or is the lack of sleep finally getting to me? "I knew I couldn't come empty-handed so..."

"You're gonna persuade me with food?" I purse my lips together, trying my utter best to hold back a laugh.

It helps, a little. But the action has Carson's eyes drifting to my lips and I don't know how to feel about it.

"It's a peace offering," he says. "My sister once said food was the equivalent of a white flag. Did I mention it was cherry?"

I stare at the pie, which looks oh-so tempting. "How do I know you're not going to throw it at my face again?"

"Holy fuck," he mutters to himself. "Are you still pressed about it? I didn't intend on hitting you, you know. Jake was right behind you. How many times do I have to apologize for it?"

"The limit does not exist," I huff.

"Well, we're making progress with calculus." He snorts before stepping back from the countertop. "I'm not touching the pie, okay? I'm leaving it right here. Do with it what you will. Just know that I'm offering to help you. No limitations, no conditions, no catch. Just volunteering my time to help a girl stay in the university she worked hard to get into."

Is he being considerate? My instincts aren't buzzing like little flies in my mind. Usually, I'm pretty good at detecting lies. I learned how to after my mom died and wasn't sure if people were genuine around me or just felt pity toward me.

The answer was always pity.

Very few people make the list of showing genuine sincerity. Carson is one of them. Apparently.

I inch closer to the countertop, closer to the fresh scent that lingers on him. This is probably the part where I agree to this right? Well, there's still one stipulation.

"What's in it for you?" The only thought that went through my mind.

If Carson's surprised by my question, then he doesn't show it. Instead, he lifts a brow. "Can't I just do something out of the goodness of my heart?"

"Nope."

He sobers up. "Cynical much?"

"Just not naive," I retort. "You have to want something." Everything goes both ways. It's not some trauma-induced cynicism. Merely just common sense, in my opinion. He offers me pie and a chance to boost my grade. I should give him something in exchange, right?

I watch Carson think about it. This is the first time I've ever really paid attention to his reactions. His brows scrunched up and after a while, he shrugs. "I got nothing."

I feel my eyebrows lift. "Nothing," I repeat.

"Nothing," he echoes. "I'm perfectly content, *Just Diana*. If anything, you'd be doing me a solid by giving me something else to do other than schoolwork, going to classes, and bothering my roommates. You can only do so much."

Why do I not believe him? I'm tempted as fuck to call Carson out on his bullshit but my sushi is starting to get warm—it's always the best when cold—and I'm really hungry, so I just dismiss it.

"Fine," I answer, just ready to get this over with. "I'll take you up on it."

He lets out a breath—of relief or something—and grabs his jacket, heading for the back door. "We start tomorrow. Meet me at the village."

"Wait, tomorrow?" I exclaim. "That's too early."

He doesn't even look back as he throws his jacket onto one shoulder. "The sooner the better, Diana," he calls out as he leaves.

Now it's my turn to take a deep breath and exhale. I'm going to be in for a long, long, few weeks.

6

Growing Tolerance
Carson

The sad part about this is that Diana was the first person to ask me what I wanted out of this tutoring gig.

No one—not even my twin sister nor my parents—has asked me what I wanted. In the past twenty years. Maybe I'm diving a little too deep into just one question or Diana cares about something regarding me.

For the first time—even if it was just a moment of relapse for her—I didn't feel like an afterthought.

Again, a little sad.

I'm sitting in the middle of the village, watching people ride on bikes, a couple of people on skateboards, or waiting in line for poke bowls. Before finding a table, I picked up a snack from Trader Joe's and started munching on the bag, headphones in, and listening to the self-titled Hozier album. With bonus tracks.

Typical Saturday for me.

I'm halfway through the bag of Trader Joe's-style spicy corn chips when Diana approaches the table with her bag slung over her shoulder, dressed in an outfit that most people wouldn't take a second glance at—just a light beige sweater and ripped blue jeans. With her? She makes it look pristine.

I pull out one headphone with my clean hand to provide my full attention.

"Sorry I'm late," she apologizes as she pulls up a chair.

I check my watch. The minute hand isn't at zero yet. "You're early." By five minutes. Not that I'm a stickler for punctuality. Sure, I'm here early as well but I got restless.

"This isn't early for me," she remarks.

Oh, she must be one of those people. The ones who are critically early to every little gathering and petrified of tardiness.

I know the type a little too well. That used to be my sister before college.

Dusting the chili powder from my hands with a finger, I reach for my backpack to grab my notebook. I pull out an orange notebook and put it back, knowing that my math notebook is red.

Math is red, orange is for the class I'm a teaching aide for, and history is green. All sciences are shades of blue. There's no other way to do it.

After rummaging through my backpack for a few more seconds, I mutter a curse under my breath as the realization that my notebook isn't there settles in. How is that even possible? I just had the class yesterday.

I try to remember where I put it and the image of it sitting at my desk back at the house has me groaning a little too loud. Fuck me, why did I do that?

"What happened now?" The brunette across the table asks.

I lift my head back up to her face, those same hazel-green eyes that are usually narrowed in my direction are softened. Not accompanied by the usual yet harsh stink-eye that's always aimed at my direction.

"I left my notes at home," I answer glumly.

She rolls her eyes at me. There's the sass I'm so accustomed to. And the stink-eye. "Way to be prepared, Ryder."

"I didn't do it on purpose," I argue, rolling my eyes back at her.

Diana then pulls out a big textbook from her bag (how she was able to fit it in there, I will never know) and puffs. Her curtain bangs fall right in front of her face and she pushes them away. "Not to fret." She gestures to the calculus textbook.

"You might be one of the few who actually look at the textbook," I snort. No one else uses the textbook because our professor doesn't go by it. He should, if I'm being honest because his teaching sucks. The only reason I'm passing this class is because I'm teaching myself more than our professor is teaching us.

"The textbook isn't helping," she retorts.

"Is it because you're also listening to Scott's lectures?" I ask with a raised brow.

"Don't you?"

I shake my head. "He says the class is hard but that's because he can't teach. I suggest not listening to him and more to the textbook."

"If you're so smart, then why don't you teach the class yourself?"

I scoff. "Because that shit's depressing." I don't want to be one of those teachers who's all sad, bald, and stuck in a love triangle with sine, cosine, and tangent. Unlike some teachers—cough, Professor Scott, cough—I'm not fucking cut out for it.

"Depressing?" she furrows her brows in confusion.

I wave it off. "Not important." I point to a paragraph on the page I opened a minute ago. "Let's start from the first chapter and go from there," I tell her. "Grab a notebook or whatever. You'll need it."

Diana does as she's told, slowly and surely. "Why from there? I thought we would only go over what we learned this week."

I shake my head at her. "Starting from the beginning gives us more of a baseline of what you need to look over. There's no point in going forward if you can't understand what you've already learned." Math is simply adding onto what you've learned before, narrowing every little thing—circles and pi, to name a few. It's always growing.

She raises a brow at me. Diana does that a lot. "I guess you do know what you're doing."

I wink. "I always know what I'm doing, *Just Diana*."

She lets out a groan and I begin the session, giving a summary of the chapter and an equation from the textbook. This goes on for a while, stopping at chapter six—where we're currently at. By then, it started getting a little chilly and the sunset already started to hide behind the buildings.

"So what's the prognosis, doc?" She asks, rubbing her right wrist unconsciously. I noticed throughout the review that Diana did that often. By often, I mean after every equation I handed her.

I wonder why.

But instead of asking, I dismiss that thought and click my tongue. "We definitely need to go over a fair amount of the material."

"Ugh, seriously?"

"Sorry to disappoint but Rome wasn't built in a day, *Just Diana*."

"But everything?" She looks back down at the textbook before looking back up to me. "Isn't that a little tedious?"

"Not everything," I correct. "Just the parts you don't understand."

"So everything."

Wow, she doubts herself a lot, doesn't she? There are small parts of each chapter that we need to look over again but that doesn't mean being nitpicky. "You are a lot smarter than you give yourself credit for. There's stuff you understand much better than others—plus, with my help, you'll be a mathematician in no time."

"Can 'no time' also equal by next week?" She adds air quotes.

I shrug. "No better time than now to get started."

"It's almost four."

I check my watch. It doesn't feel like four o'clock. "Time went by fast."

"Yeah."

"Are you working tomorrow?"

Diana shakes her head, her wispy curtain bangs slapping her face. "We start tomorrow, then?"

I nod. "Same time, same place."

"Alright." She packs her supplies and lifts her bag onto her shoulder—using her left hand instead of her right, which is a good thing—and before she can walk away from the table, I call out her name. She turns around with a puzzled look on her face.

"Just," I begin. "Don't lose hope, okay?"

Diana doesn't respond. Instead, she studies me for a good minute before turning back around and walking away.

I find myself watching until a group of around ten people walks in my line of sight.

7

Can't Believe I'm Doing This

Diana

After pressing play on my phone and allowing the sounds of The Weeknd to fill my ears, I continue my walk from the tutoring session, somewhat disappointed in myself for how little progress I've made in my work. My schoolwork is something I pride myself on being good at but now, I'm not entirely sure.

I hate it—the idea of not knowing. Not being able to prepare myself or having another backup plan.

When I find my house coming up on the street, I quicken my pacing until I reach the front porch, enter the passcode for the door, and open it to find all of my roommates scattered around the living room.

Lucia is at the table, painting her nails a deep green. Emma is reading a book—a romance novel I assume, based on the front cover—while her cousin Ronnie is eating a slice of pie and watching something on his laptop.

"Hey," I say, staring at the half-eaten slice of pie on his plate. "Is that from my pie?" I didn't even get to eat it yet.

Ronnie looks up from his laptop, eyes wide. "Shit, I thought it was Lucia's."

"It's cherry pie, dumbass," Lucia comments. "No one else in this house loves cherry-flavored anything like Diana."

"She's right," I point out. "I do love cherries." In fact, so much so that I predict whatever children I end up having far into the future will love it as much as I, if not more.

"Hey, where's Madi?" I ask, not finding our fifth roommate in the sitting area. With perfect timing, the gentle sounds of her violin are heard, flowing into the windows. She's a music performance major and during the weekends—when she's not in orchestra practice—she practices outside.

The guys don't mind it, just as long as she isn't practicing at night and there aren't any parties thrown in the yard between our houses. It doesn't happen that often, these days—the partying, not Madi's involuntary violin recitals in the yard.

"Where did you get the pie, anyway?" Ronnie questions.

I just shrug and respond with, "A friend gave it to me."

"Does that friend happen to live in the house behind us?" He grins.

Without responding, I take the fork out of his hand and snatch a bite for myself, nearing moaning in delight from how good it tastes. How is the crust so flaky? And the filling...don't even get me started on that.

"Well, there's my answer," he mutters. "Whatever happened to your whole 'never associate with the enemy' mindset?"

Lucia looks up from her nails so fast that I wonder how she doesn't have whiplash. "Did you finally talk to him about it?"

That has our fourth roommate looking up from her book—which is a feat all on its own because Emma is attached to her books—with brown eyes lit up like a fire. "Is Diana finally dating someone?"

"I'm not dating anyone, Emma," I clarify. "My scholarship's in jeopardy and I need help with a class."

"So I suggested asking someone in the class to help," Lucia adds. "Looks like you took my advice, D."

I am about to correct her before Emma speaks up, and I close my mouth since she hardly contributes to the conversation given her social anxiety. She's more of a listener and enjoys receiving gossip than spreading it around.

"This should be interesting," Emma remarks.

"I'll bet," Ronnie agrees with his cousin. "Let's see how long she'll last before ripping his head off."

I turn to Ronnie with furrowed brows. "How do you know who it is?"

"Enzo said something about it this morning."

"Are you guys official yet?" Lucia asks, edging closer to her seat.

Pressing his lips with a ring-clad thumb, Ronnie shrugs with a mischievous glint in his eyes. "I don't kiss and tell."

I gasp in delight. Thank fucking god. Those two have been hooking up since September and he has not said shit about their status.

"He did invite me to this house party," he continues. "It's tonight. You guys down to join?"

"I'm down," Emma responds. "Someone go talk to Madi."

"I'll relay her the info," I offer. "There's no point in my going but I might as well be useful."

"Come on, D!" Ronnie exclaims. "This one's supposed to be chill. Just an outdoor party."

"You know how I feel about parties," I remind him.

"We know how you feel about *drinking*," Lucia corrects me.

I raise both eyebrows at her. "You know what parties lead to?"

"Optional drinking, duh." She paints one last coat of polish on her nails before blowing on them.

"Not at this school," I mutter. Parties at USC are intense, from what I hear—again, I've never been to one—and there's a reason I stay away from them. One thing about this school I didn't take into account was the partying culture, especially on Greek row.

Parties lead to drinking, which leads to bad decisions and death. I've already nearly died once and I prefer to stay alive until I'm at least eighty, thank you very much.

"It's not a frat party this time," Ronnie reminds me. "So it shouldn't be as crazy."

"I'm going outside." I walk out to Madi's practice and she doesn't stop. How someone can shut out the world around them, I'll never know. But that's what she always does.

Madi stops after a minute and puts her bow and instrument down so she can stretch. Just as she's twisting her back, she spots me watching. Her amber eyes go wide since she's not used to people watching her. "How long have you been standing there?"

"Just got here," I assure her. "Ronnie and Lucia wanted to let you know about a party they got invited to."

Madi starts cracking her knuckles, a nervous tick of hers. "Is it another Greek row party?"

I shake my head.

"Are you going?"

I shake it again. "You know how I feel about parties." Madi doesn't frequent nearly as many parties as the rest of our roommates because she's more focused on practicing. She still shows up here and there but doesn't succumb to any personal trauma she might have.

Good for her.

"Yeah, but I don't know why," she points out. "Anytime drinking is mentioned you get tense." Madi then points to my wrists. "Like you are now. Reminds me of how I act before a recital."

Looking down, I notice how my nails dig into the palms of my hands. My right wrist doesn't hurt as much as it did back at my first session with Carson, luckily. I hate when my old injuries flare up but I've managed.

Releasing my fingers, I shrug. "So? It's no big deal."

Madi gives me a look as if she's saying, *really, girl?* "I know you don't want to talk about it, but you don't need to drink to have fun. I don't."

My eyebrows fly up to my hairline. "Really?"

"I hate the taste of alcohol," she explains, wrinkling her nose. "And Adrian doesn't drink much, either, so I always hang out with him when the others are drunk off their asses." At the mention of Adrian, her face turns slightly red.

"How about this," she suggests. "You can hang out with me when the others start going crazy, and I'll keep an eye on you."

The fact that I am considering this is crazy to me. I don't know what that says about me; the fact that I'm thinking about going to a party when I haven't even attended one nor hosted one of any kind since I was thirteen.

"Are you sure about this?" I ask wearily.

Madi nods and I find myself giving in. "I'll go."

8

My Spontaneous Sister

Carson

My sister is nothing but spontaneous.

It's something that sets us apart from being twins. I'm the more organized one, while she's a bit on the wild side, and a lot more unhinged. Here's an example.

About five minutes after I arrive back from the village, Carly makes her way through the front gate and to the yard, where she and Adrian are seated on the lawn chairs, probably talking about movies or something.

They look a little too friendly, in my opinion.

I open the front door of my house, holding my hands up to my mouth like a megaphone. "Yo, Miller! Stop flirting with my sister!"

My buddy's head turns in my direction and groans. "For the last time, I am not interested in your sister like that."

I know that, but it's so easy to tease Adrian.

"Your loss, A," Carly sighs. She's joking. Carly doesn't date—she has guys, but never boyfriends—and it's always been that way. Some say she's flighty, while I believe that nobody is entertaining enough for her. "I'm a real catch."

"Car, what are you doing here?" I ask.

"I sent you a text," she tells me. "Didn't you get it?"

"You never sent me anything," I assure her.

Grabbing her phone from the back pocket of her shorts, she stares at the screen with brows furrowed. "Huh, I guess I didn't. I swear I typed something."

"Carly…"

"Can't I just check on my little brother?" She stands up from her seat and heads over to sling an arm over my shoulders and pulls me in

36

for a side hug. She's not that much shorter than me so her arm rests comfortably. We also look fairly alike for a pair of fraternal twins, except my hair is darker than hers. "Let me see how my little Cars is doing."

"Little?" I groan. "I'm taller."

"But you're not older," she shoots back, a smug grin that has me rolling my eyes. "Whatcha boys up to?"

"Nothing," I answer, while Adrian responds with, "We're heading to this party later tonight. It's supposed to be pretty chill."

Really, Adrian? You don't bring up the p-word in front of my sister. If anything, that word should be spelt-out but Carly's so fucking smart she would figure it out in an instant.

Her pale blue eyes light up at the word and she gasps. "I'm in! This is going to be fun!"

"But it's supposed to be chill," I say.

Carly scoffs. "It's a USC party. How chill can they get?"

$$3 \, . \, 1 \, 4 \, 1 \, 5 \, 9 \, 2 \, 6 \, 5 \, 3 \, 5 \, 9$$

She's not wrong.

I've partied a fair amount in my time here but I haven't attended other college parties—just the ones held at USC. Just because it doesn't have a whole bunch of Greek letters attached to the front of the house doesn't mean it won't be intense.

Must be the stress of the midterms ending that has people going batshit crazy.

Once we entered the house, the rest of us split. Everyone but me and Adrian went in different directions from each other. I'm nursing a lukewarm can of Sprite while watching a game of beer pong go wrong through a window outside, while Adrian's drinking a water because he's too much of a lightweight who easily gets buzzed after one beer—which he chugged and regretted almost immediately.

"Oh look." Adrian's head is turned towards the front door. "The others are here."

I'm about to ask who he's talking about when Ronnie Cho wraps his arms around the both of us. "What's up, cocksuckers?"

"Enzo's running late," Adrian replies. Not even a hello that precedes it. Why is he even broodier when buzzed? It's insane.

"How did you know what I was going to ask, dear Millie?"

"Not Millie," he complains. The dude hates that nickname.

Allowing myself to turn around, I spot the rest of Enzo's roommates. What surprises me more is finding Diana here. Even though I know she doesn't attend these parties, that's not what catches me off-guard.

It's how she's dressed. Don't get me wrong, she looks fucking beautiful—always has since the day I met her—but tonight...wow.

Even my inside thoughts are drawing blanks to describe her. Her hair flows down her shoulders and over the thin straps of her cherry-red top and slightly faded shorts and I can't help but stare.

She almost commands my attention.

"Uh, Carson?"

Blinking, I turn around to see Adrian and Ronnie staring at me with somewhat concerned expressions.

"Yeah?" I raise a brow.

"You didn't hear what I asked?" Ronnie smirks. "Of course you didn't. Can you stop eye-fucking my roommates, please? The world would be better for it."

Adrian takes this moment to shrug out of Ronnie's arm. "I need another drink." He stalks off without another glance back. Odd, he hardly ever drinks to begin with but he must be *nervous* about this undisclosed girl.

Ronnie and I share a glance and he shrugs. "He's your roommate, Ryder," he reminds me—not that I need it—before releasing me from his grasp and walking away in the opposite direction.

Here I am, left alone while everyone else continues to party. Maybe I've outgrown the party scene. Ditching the drink on an island, I reach for an open cooler and grab a soda can. I'm not even slightly buzzed but it's the taste of beer that I need to wash away.

"Carrrrssssssonnnnn," my sister slurs, wrapping one arm around my back. "I lost my ring," she wails.

And my sister, the lightweight that she is, is already drunk. *Oh, someone please help me.*

"Wait," I say, prying my sister off of me and standing the both of us upright. "You lost the ring?"

She nods, a single tear slipping down her cheek. "I can't find it anywhere!"

Great. Carly and I both have Irish Claddagh rings that were gifted to us back when we graduated high school from our late grandmother. I never lost mine but Carly has a habit of misplacing everything she touches. It's not her fault, usually.

"Where did you last see it?" I ask her slowly, enunciating each word because I've been around a drunk Carly before—and it's not easy.

"It was on my hand for one minute," she tells me. "And in the next, it's gone. I don't see it anywhere."

Observing the groups, I take a look around. Carly's ring is small so it won't be easy to spot it from a distance.

"What do I do?" She cries. That ring is important to my sister so I can understand how upset she is. The Claddagh ring holds a lot of sentimental value to her.

"Car," I repeat over and over again to calm her down. "We're going to find it, don't you worry. We just need to keep looking."

Wherever that fucking ring may be.

9

Weirdest Night Yet

Diana

This party is so not worth a Saturday night in my best party dress.

Or, outfit, in this case. Just a red top that I think might be too tight on me paired with some shorts and sneakers. After telling Lucia that I chose to attend, she got so excited and started rummaging through her closet for something I could wear. When we finally decided on this, she said—a direct quote, mind you—"Aphrodite who?" While touching up my lipstick.

When the rest of us walked into the house where the party is held, I understood why Madi didn't go to a lot of the parties. This is the kind of party where you'd have to be extremely drunk to have fun. Dionysus would disapprove.

Maybe sticking to Madi is a good idea.

I nudge her shoulder. "Do you want to do anything?"

Her amber eyes move around the entrance area, to the living room, and the little entranceway that I'm pretty sure leads to the kitchen—this is a big house—until her eyes land on a tall figure leaning against a wall, nursing a water bottle.

How cliche can college get? I could turn this whole scenario into a college romance novel and make billions off of it—and I don't even read romance.

"What about table tennis?" Madi takes my hand and guides me outside to the big ping-pong table.

After bumping into multiple tipsy college students, we finally make it out alive. I go to the opposite side of the table, grab the paddle and ball in front of me, and hold it out. "You ready to lose, Mads?"

She narrows her eyes in a challenging manner. "What makes you think you're gonna win, Diana?"

I make the first serve and she reciprocates by hitting the white ping pong ball with a smack. Maybe this party could be fun, as long as there's table tennis. We go at it for a while, until I miss the ball and it goes bouncing on the table and practically flies away.

"Point for me," Madi says with a smile on her face.

"Well played," I acknowledge because I refuse to act like a sore loser.

Before Madi can respond, Adrian comes up to us. "Woah, Diana. You're here." He then turns to Madi with a joking grin, which is odd for the broody guy. "How much money did they pay her?"

She giggles. Okay, something is up with these two. "Nothing, I swear."

Taking it as my cue, I turn around slowly to retrieve the ball. The more steps I take, the less uneasy I feel about being a third wheel.

I bump into a tall, buff figure. Before I can apologize, said figure holds out his hand—I've determined that it's a guy—where the little white ball rests.

Looking up, I find Mason staring down at me. I may not interact with all my neighbors but Mason is the one I see the least of. "Thanks, Mason," I reply, grabbing the ball from his hand.

"No problem," he grunts. "Never thought I'd see you here, Diana."

"Neither did anyone else," I mutter.

He nods, then swivels his head from left to right before turning back to me. "Did Lucia come with you?"

"Yeah, she's with Emma and Ronnie while they wait for Enzo."

"Thanks." Mason then dashes off. Okay, what is it with all of my roommates getting with our neighbors? First, there's Ronnie and Enzo—no one was surprised there, to be honest—then Adrian and Madi, and now Mason and Lucia?

I fear I might die alone with thirteen cats at this rate but I digress.

Turning back around, I make my way over to the ping pong table when I step on something round and hard, nearly falling onto the floor. Luckily, I manage to catch myself before I can face-plant on the freshly cut grass.

What did I step on? It wasn't a Lego—that thing felt much more painful than a Lego ever did. I crouch down, trying my utter best to keep myself covered with my dress while also getting low enough, and picking up the silver ring. Not sanitary. I drop the ball onto the table and head back inside to find the nearest sink.

Because I have such amazing luck (apparently), I find a lack of college students waiting for the bathroom and it only takes me two minutes to enter inside and wash the dirt off of the ring.

Now it's time to find the owner. When I was younger, I always had a habit of finding lost things and returning them to their owners. Like a Cuban Tinkerbell in the first movie, or Hermes.

I chuckle to myself. With the ring in my hand, I look like I'm about to propose to someone but that couldn't be further from the truth.

A couple of minutes pass by and I have yet to hear a single person drunkenly scream, "Where's my ring?"

"Where's my ring???"

There it is.

But I can't pinpoint the sound to anyone in particular so I head on over to the kitchen and lean my head against the freezer door. I allow myself to observe the ring resting on the palm of my right hand. In the middle of the silver band rests two hands holding a heart, with a crown on the top.

I recognize this design. I've never seen a Claddagh ring in person before until now and let's just say that the pictures I've found scourging the internet don't do it justice. Luckily, it doesn't look damaged anywhere so it's safe to say that my Converse didn't destroy them.

"Hey, don't worry about it, Carly. You can tell Mom about it and she'll understand." The hairs on my arm stand up as I listen to the soothing voice that I've come to know too well. After all, the owner of the voice has been living in the house behind me for the past two months.

"I can't, Carson," an unfamiliar voice cries. "You know how mad she'll be when she finds out."

"Let's just get you some water, okay? Sober you up a little and then we'll talk more about it."

"Okay."

I push myself off the refrigerator and fiddle with the ring, pretending that I didn't just listen to his uber-short conversation. It's not my business, after all.

"Diana?" *Mierda.*

Maybe I can pretend that I didn't hear him. No, that won't work because I'm terrible at acting. I can try.

"I know you heard me."

I make a mental note to never audition for any future movies before slowly turning around to find his blue eyes on me. Carson's not alone either—he's holding up a girl with very similar features as him and lighter hair. A very drunk, girl version of him.

Oh great, there's two of them.

"Uh, hi," I laugh nervously. "What are you doing here?"

Before he can respond, the girl next to him widens her equally blue eyes and points to my hand. "Oh my gosh, where did you find it?"

I was so aware of Carson that I forgot about the Claddagh ring I'm holding. Holding it out to her, I respond with, "Found it on the grass."

"Thank you!!!" The girl lets go of Carson, stumbling slightly towards me so she can wrap me in a hug.

A flimsy, beer-scented hug.

She's slightly taller than I am but it's surprisingly not uncomfortable, just unexpected. Eyes wide, I look at Carson, who shrugs.

My eyes turn into little slits with the way I glare at him.

"I don't know you but I already love you!" She lets go of me to slip the ring back onto her right finger. "I could have sworn someone had stolen it by now. You didn't want this all to yourself?"

It's now my turn to shrug. "Though it's pretty, I'm more of a gold girl."

She gives me a once-over before shaking her head. "You would look good in silver, too," she remarks before turning to Carson. "Don't you think?"

His cheeks turn visibly red and he stutters. "Uh, sure thing."

Is it just me or does he look as uncomfortable with the predicament as I feel?

Choosing not to subject myself to this any longer, I reach for the fridge, grab a soda can, and hastily exit the kitchen without another word.

I think I've had enough of this party. Or any party for the foreseeable future.

When I reach the living room yet again, the first thing I spot is a set of long, black braids that I recognize are Lucia's. I tap her shoulder and she whips around, a couple of braids hitting my arm. "What's up, girl?"

Okay, she's not drunk yet but Lucia's not a lightweight, either, so it's hard to guess how many shots she's taken.

"I'm heading out," I shout through the painfully loud music.

Lucia puts her drink down. "I'll go with you."

Shaking my head, I say, "No, don't let me stop you from having more fun. I'll be fine." Looking over her shoulder, I notice Mason glancing in our direction before he quickly looks away. Yeah, that guy's got it real fucking bad. "Besides, you've got Mason to keep you company."

My best friend looks over her shoulder to find Mason and I swear her cheeks turn red. And is that giggling I hear?

There's a time and a place for me to be around those two, and right now isn't the moment.

"I'll call you an Uber," she says. In an instant, I can feel my stomach shriveling up at the mention of a car. Oh fuck no. I'll risk my chances doing anything but sitting in a car.

"I can just walk home," I assure her before turning around and squeezing through the crowds without hearing a protest come from Lucia's mouth. Briskly walk towards the front door like I'm inching closer and closer to the finish line.

Before my hand can reach the doorknob, a body knocks into me and I'm pushed away. "Sorry!" A familiar drunken voice calls out.

At least I'm not on grass again.

I check my top for any creases, and my shoes for any stains, and just as I get the all-clear, I open my mouth to apologize when Carson's voice stops me.

"You need some fresh air, too?"

I shake my head. "Going home. I'll see you later."

I reach for the doorknob a second time before he places his hand over mine. I turn my head to face him with eyes wide, not expecting the motion whatsoever. Or the small zap, which causes me to draw my right hand back in an instant and meet his gaze.

"All by yourself?" His brows furrow in...concern.

Concern? You've got to be kidding me.

I shrug. "So?" I make this journey in the dark multiple times—from school to home, work to home, study session to home, to name a few—and I haven't had many problems, except for a homeless dude on crack, chasing me for food back in August but it's not out of the ordinary for me. I'm from Miami, Florida.

Need I say more?

"At midnight?"

"What's with all the questions, Carson? Can't you save them for our next tutoring session?"

"There won't be a session if you walk home alone and get attacked by a fucking creep! And I may be an asshole in your eyes but I refuse to let you walk home alone."

"Creep?" I roll my eyes. "I'm more in danger of getting attacked by you than a homeless dude on crack, given how much I've been seeing you today alone."

"That doesn't mean I'm letting you walk home alone," he argues.

Crossing my arms over my chest, I reply, "I can take care of myself, Carson."

"I do not doubt that, *Just Diana*." He runs one hand through his light brown locks hastily. "But there's no point when I'm already heading in the same direction."

"Already?" The girl next to him whines. "But it's just getting fun."

I think amid this conversation, we forgot that she was still here. We both turn our heads to her and it's then I notice how close our faces are.

All it would take is for either of us to move even a centimeter closer...

I take a step back, putting some space between us. Maybe the hot air inside this house is getting to me and I really need some fresh air. So I grab the door while he's distracted with who I assume is his sister and step outside, immediately getting hit by the chill, mid-October breeze.

"Thank fuck," I mutter to myself. I check my pockets for my phone and realize that I had left it charging in my room. I let out a groan and run a hand through the ends of my hair.

I guess that means...

Carson and that girl (I seriously don't know her name) walk right out and when his eyes find me waiting by the door, he gestures with his free hand to follow.

"Fine," I mutter and walk behind them.

One minute, I'm annoyed by Carson's chivalry, and the next, I'm following him around like a lost nymph.

Boys are so fucking complicated.

10

Late Night Walks

Carson

I truly didn't think she was gonna say yes.

Technically, she didn't say yes but I got a mumbled agreement out of her mouth as she started following me and a drunk Carly—who is slung over my shoulder, laughing her ass off at a squirrel that just wandered by—back to my house.

Since Carly is in no shape to drive back to her apartment, I'm taking her back to my house to sober her up and let her sleep it off. After spending the entire summer break stressing out about post-production for her film that premiered on Friday, she deserved to let loose and have some fun until her next project.

"I get knocked down, but I get up again," Carly sings drunkenly while dancing. "You're never gonna get me down!"

"Shhhh!" I cover her mouth with my one free hand. "You're gonna wake up half the neighborhood!"

She bites my hand, causing me to yank it away. "What the fuck, Carly!"

I hear snickering come from behind us and when I turn around, Diana is covering her mouth with her hand, her shoulders shaking as she walks.

"Wow," I tease. "So you only laugh when it's at my expense."

Diana doubles over in laughter. "I'm not a sadist, I swear," she claims, still laughing like it's breathing for her.

"You're still laughing."

The three of us reach a stop light. Diana presses the button and we wait for the little white stick figure to appear so we can cross the street.

"She just reminds me of my little sister," Diana says as we stand by the edge of the crosswalk.

I raise a brow. "You have sisters, too?"

"Just one," she corrects, fidgeting with her wrist. Is that some sort of nervous tick?

"I'm sorry, I can't help it. Is your hand okay?"

Just as the question leaves my mouth, both her hands fall to her sides. "It's nothing."

"Doesn't seem like nothing. You do that a lot for it to be nothing, *Just Diana*."

She shrugs. "It's just an old injury flare-up. No big deal."

My eyes widen in shock. Even my fairly drunk twin sister finds that insane because she whips her head in Diana's direction. "I'm sorry, what?"

Just an old injury flare-up? Coming from a kinesiology major, injuries are not something one should downplay.

"It's really not a big deal," Diana assures us.

Carly turns to me with her dilated pupils, trying to see how I'm going to react.

"That's not what I would call it."

"What would you call it then, Doc?" Diana crosses both hands over her chest.

I've injured myself on multiple occasions in the past and I've associated a flare-up with two things: a real fucking bad injury or one that just never healed properly. She put me on the spot—and that's not something I'm very familiar with.

Thankfully, the white stick figure flashes before I'm able to answer and I can switch the topic. "We should probably cross."

"You know," Carly slurs as I wrap one of her arms around my shoulders and guide her drunk self across the street. "You look a whole lot like Ana De Armas."

"Who?" I ask.

"How are we related, Little Cars?"

I sigh. Do I really *have* to go over the logistics of how my twin sister and I came to be? Nope, I refuse to do so. "Carly, you seriously need some–"

But she refuses to listen. Instead, points to a stand in front of us. "Ooh! Tacos! We should get some."

"Uh, Carly," Diana interjects. "I don't think it's open at this hour."

As we approach the stand, we find that Diana's wrong. The truck is open and active without anyone waiting in line.

My sister turns to me, with wide blue eyes and lips out like a begging puppy. "Can we get some, Carson? Please?"

As if I'm asking for approval, my gaze moves over to Diana. She's been walking to my far left, where my sister stands (or rather, hobbles) between us. That girl is willingly forcing space between us.

At least it's only physical space. Diana isn't avoiding any topic of conversation (that will be the day) because she responds with, "The tacos could sober her up."

That settles it. We're getting tacos.

The three of us approach the truck and list our order order, with Diana getting extra cilantro on hers. I shiver at the words, "extra cilantro," but don't say a word until she tries to pay with a wallet that I didn't even know she was carrying.

I interject and try to stop Diana from paying but the girl is a strong fighter. "I am completely fine with paying, Carson!"

"Nope," I insist, resisting her shove. "I'm not letting you pay."

"Carson!"

I honestly feel bad for the guy running the truck but at least he's enjoying the show. Eventually, I sneak around by putting both hands on Diana's waist and turning her around so I can scan my card.

We wait a few more minutes before the guy brings out three plates of tacos.

"I've never seen a couple fight over a payment before," the taco guy remarks.

"We're not a couple," Diana and I say simultaneously. The two of us exchange a glance, and I swear her cheeks turn as red as her lipstick. She hands me the plate that has considerably less cilantro and walks back to Carly, who sits on the sidewalk—or rather lays—and hums to a song I'm not familiar with.

I sit down next to her and munch on the first taco, nearly moaning in delight at how good it is. Man, I missed eating tacos.

The three of us eat in silence. Carly is the first to finish and she seems to have sobered up a lot in comparison to how she was when we ordered the tacos. After a minute, she stands up and wipes her hands on her grass-stained jeans. "I'm gonna get us some napkins."

Placing my last taco down, I get up too. "Should you still be—"

"Don't worry little Cars," she calls back, already making her way back to the taco stand. "I can take care of myself."

I sit back down.

"Little Cars?" Diana asks, with her grin still in place. If I knew it would take tacos for her to not act so standoffish around me, I would have showed up at her back door every day with a plate of them. Extra cilantro and all.

But I groan at the nickname. "She's one of those people who doesn't let go of the fact that she's older than you."

"Is it a big age difference?"

I shake my head. "Try five minutes."

She winces. "That's rough, doc."

"A little." I finish my last taco and put the white paper plate in the empty spot that Carly occupied. "I'm used to it."

"Doesn't it bother you?" She takes another bite of her taco. "The nickname?"

I shrug. "Not really, anymore."

"Really?" Her brows furrow. "It would bother me if I were you."

"It did," I tell her. Carly isn't ill-minded—except for the ADHD—but her nicknames sometimes show how much she cares.

"What did?" Carly asks as she sits herself back down. I quickly grab my empty plate before she reaches the cold concrete, somewhat soberer than thirty seconds ago.

"Eh, nothing important," I dismiss.

She eyes me before whipping her head towards Diana, who polishes off her last taco and folds the paper plate in half. "You ready?"

"Sober already after three tacos?" I laugh.

We stand up and continue the journey. "Nah, I'm still drunk as hell," Carly laughs. "Do you really think a few tacos would sober me up completely? Oh, Little Cars, you are so naive."

"Well, neither of us drink," Diana interjects. "So how would we know?"

Carly shrugs and starts singing that song again as we continue the walk home. One thing my sister sucks at is singing, so I try not to laugh at her so-called singing abilities—I also can't sing to save my life so who am I to judge?

I glance at Diana and her eyes are filled with laughter. Yeah, she's trying not to laugh as well.

I smile to myself. She's starting to tolerate me a whole lot more. It gives me hope that we can get through the rest of the tutoring sessions.

"Oh, thanks by the way," she tells me.

"For what?"

"Paying for the food." She tucks a stray hair behind her ear. "You didn't have to do that."

"Funny how you thought I would let you pay," I smirk, which causes her to let out a laugh.

Yeah, I think we'll be fine.

$$3 . 1 4 1 5 9 2 6 5 3 5 9$$

"How the fuck am I supposed to remember this?" She exclaims angrily, a little too loud for the study room we're in.

Our sessions have been going off without a hitch for the last few days but the moment we reached optimization, all hell broke loose. To be fair, out of everything we've learned in this class, optimization was my least favorite. It's the literal hell we've been fighting over.

Today, we had only thirty minutes to go over this topic because we both had to work. I may have finished assisting with a class for the evening but Diana has a night shift at the library so we took some time during her break to start looking over a new chapter that we will continue tomorrow.

"The context of the problem," I try to explain. "The arch is the same as a parabola that opens down." I draw it on the whiteboard, pointing to the curved end. "This is the midpoint."

"Ohh," she groans, rubbing her wrist for the umpteenth time. Some people rub their heads when math troubles them—Diana Blanco rubs her wrist. Singular, because it's always her right wrist and never the left. "I hate word problems."

"Me too," I agree.

"We better get a cheat sheet of equations." Diana lets go of her wrist. "There's no way we're expected to remember any of this like last time. No wonder everyone else failed. Speaking of…" Her gaze meets mine with curiosity. "How did you not fail?"

"It's not a big deal, *Just Diana*," I answer.

"You managed to remember all of those equations for the midterm just because? I don't believe that. You don't have a super brain or something. Do you?"

So I've never had trouble remembering a lot of things growing up. That's just how I've been. But I've never been asked about it before until now. "It's eidetic."

Diana raises a brow, clearly not knowing what it means.

"It doesn't take a lot for me to remember details," I explain.

"So, you have a photographic memory?"

"No. I can still forget things."

She wrinkles her nose in this adorable manner. "Man, you're lucky. If I had an eidetic memory, I wouldn't be struggling with this stupid class."

"My memory is not getting me an A in this class." I'm running on sheer luck, expensive-ass coffee, and a small will to live.

She scoffs, crossing her arms. "Yeah, right. You and your pretty little eidetic brain are breezing through this class just fine."

I raise a brow curiously. "Oh, so you think I'm pretty?"

She narrows her hazel eyes at me, and I swear I saw a tinge of pink in those cheeks. "Really? That's all you heard?"

I chuckle at her frustration—she's cute when she's annoyed—but before I can say anything else, a knock on the study room door shifts her attention from me. Through the windows, I notice a very tall guy with dreadlocks and deep bronze skin, standing next to a cart of books. "Hey, D. Lottie said your break ended ten minutes ago."

"*Mierda*," she mutters to herself. "I gotta go." She starts packing up her things.

"When does your shift end?" I ask her.

She freezes in her chair for a minute before answering me. "Ten-thirty. Why?"

I check my phone, looking at the time. It's only about two hours from now, so I can get a whole lot of work done if I focus hard enough while I wait. "No reason."

"You're not waiting for me, are you? I've told you many times, Carson. You don't have to do that."

"But I'm offering," I assure her. "Besides, it's dark out and you shouldn't have to walk home alone."

Her face softens and she doesn't say another word before grabbing her bag and walking out the door. The guy waiting there eyes me like the newest edition of a book before turning around and following behind Diana, pushing the cart of books with him.

I stay for as long as required before packing up my things and moving over to an empty table out in the open.

Looking back at the textbook equations, I groan internally.

At least I'm trying, D.

11

I Don't Know This Feeling

Diana

"I thought we hated him," Roman says as we walk away from the study room I spent my entire break in.

"Well, things have changed," I announce as I grab the first two books on top of Roman's cart and shove them onto the shelves. I didn't even look at the author's name or the genre. Athena—the goddess of wisdom—would be outraged.

"It's been two weeks—surely your mind didn't change like that." He snaps his fingers.

"Again," I reiterate, turning to face my friend. "Things have changed."

He snorts. "They sure changed real fast, especially for you. A girl set in your ways."

Roman's right about one thing: I am pretty set on my ways. For me, if I feel something about it, then that's it. Not much can change my opinion and I'd do anything to defend it.

"He's just helping me with a class, that's all," I tell him as I grab books and place them neatly on the shelves. "After I pass, I can go back to ignoring him most of the time."

"Or, maybe you like spending time with the guy."

I shake my head vehemently. "Not possible. I just want to get this over with." Passing my math class is currently my main priority. All of my other classes this semester pertain to my classics major.

Would it be crazy to say that I don't mind the sessions Carson and I have been doing? Carson's a lot smarter than I had pegged him to be. I know it's rude for me to assume anything about his intellect but the guy doesn't participate in class.

54

Plus, he tutors at a pace I'm comfortable with. He ensures I understand what we've just reviewed before moving on to the next chapter. That says a lot in comparison to our *actual* professor, who makes me question how he still holds a position at this school.

So, yeah. Roman might just be right about me liking how goofy Carson can get sometimes. I'd go as far as to claim that it's almost...adorable.

But I digress.

"If it helps," Roman continues. "The feeling is mutual."

I turn to face him, brushing my curtain bangs away from my face. "What?"

"Carl."

"Carson."

He dismisses it with a wave of his hand. "Whatever his name is. Pie guy. That fucker is such a flirt."

I chuckle. "He doesn't flirt and not with me."

"It's not okay to be blind to it, Diana," he teases. "I'd suggest getting glasses so you can see better."

I scoff. "My vision is fine." I shove another book in between two paperbacks and wince when I see the covers fold slightly, leading me to mend it as best as I can.

"If it helps, I also need glasses." When I raise a brow, he responds with, "To help me notice all the red flags that I should avoid at all fucking costs."

We bust out laughing before Lottie shushes us from her desk. That woman has superhearing or something.

Roman and I get through the final two hours of my shift before I sign myself out. He still has to work a few more hours. I don't envy him.

Once I'm out of the breakroom, I head up the stairs and immediately spot Carson at a table nearby. The common study area of the library is—for the most part—empty and unsettlingly quiet for a Thursday night. This is actually when I find most people pulling all-nighters to finish papers.

As I approach Carson's table, I notice one thing and one thing only: he's asleep.

His head rests on the table, strands of hair in front of his eyes. I inch closer to the table, careful not to wake him up. As I quietly sit down on an empty chair, I quickly become aware of his soft breathing patterns. It's almost peaceful.

He looks kind of adorable when he doesn't notice.

Dammit, Diana! You should not be thinking about your tutor like that.

I don't think about anyone like that. It's not that I have anything against crushes at all—I've had them before and even a couple of fleeting relationships—romance was something I've never put my all into. I've come to accept that I'm just not a hopeless romantic, and there's nothing wrong with it.

Something on his right hand catches my eye. As I inspect, I notice it's another Claddagh ring. I'll admit: I may or may not have looked up Claddagh rings after Carson dropped me off at my house. Only because I was curious—no other reason behind it.

The band is much thicker than his sister's was that night I found it and the band is rimmed with silver, with the hands-holding-a-heart symbol in the center. What I learned from that impromptu Google search is what it could mean, depending on how you wear it—specifically your relationship status.

If Carson wears his the way it is now—on the ring finger of his right hand with the bottom of the heart facing outwards—then it means he's single.

I shove that tidbit of information towards the back of my head as his eyes start to flutter open. He takes a while to come to his surroundings before his eyes settle on me and he smirks lazily. "You checking me out, *Just Diana?*"

I can't resist an eye roll. "In your dreams, Ryder."

"Don't worry, I know how handsome I am."

"And you're humble, too," I mutter. This guy...

Checking his watch, he grabs his notebook and bag and we stand up at the same time. "You ready to go?"

I nod and follow him down the stairs. Normally, on walks home, I play music to fill the silence and avoid talking to random people but it would be rude of me if I pulled out my headphones and started listening to Frank Ocean or One Direction.

So we walk in silence, which doesn't seem to bother me at all. It's quite comforting until I feel my wrist tense up as we cross the street.

Ugh, why now? It happens way too often these days. Granted, I spent the entire day taking notes and shelving books with my dominant hand. It didn't like that.

Stupid, stubborn bones that never healed properly and refuses to.

When this happens, I just carefully massage it. It may not be the right thing to do but it helps alleviate the pain.

This is the exact moment Carson glances in my direction. More specifically, my wrist. "It still hurts?"

I shrug. "From time to time."

We arrive at the front porch of my house. The lights are on inside, which doesn't surprise me—all of my roommates are night owls—but I don't move to the front door.

"Thanks," I tell him before walking up the steps to the front door.

"Wait one second," Carson tells me before walking towards the gate that separates the front year from the back and disappears.

Okay, what?

Puzzled, I twist the doorknob and waltz inside my house. Yeah, it's already chilly outside and the Floridian in me has yet to adjust to the quote-on-quote perfect weather Los Angeles has to provide. There's no way I'm staying out there.

I toss my bag onto the couch, which startles Emma slightly. "Sorry," I apologize.

She shrugs and resumes her typing. "Don't worry."

I make myself more comfortable in the living room—by grabbing a cherry soda and sipping on it as I scroll through my phone. My brain needs a break from learning and it always comes in the form of mindlessly scrolling through social media like the girl that I am.

Five minutes later, someone knocks on the back door. Emma and I look up from our respective screens and glance at each other.

"Were you expecting someone?" She questions.

I shake my head. "You?"

"No, that's why I asked."

We stare at the back door for a minute before another trio of knocks is heard.

"Who's gonna open it?"

Emma scoots her chair back, a bit away from the front door. There's my answer. Emma Allen isn't known for being extroverted. She's one of the most timid party people I've ever encountered. I don't dwell on that when I stand up and open the door.

Instead, I dwell on the fact that Carson's standing right in front of me, holding a black splint with a wry grin. "I thought I told you to wait."

"It's fifty degrees outside," I retort. "No way in hell I was gonna wait any longer outside." Not when heaters and air conditioning exist.

He chuckles softly. "You don't tolerate a lot, do you?"

"Not true. I tolerate your bullshit."

"What are you talking about?" He arches a brow, and the stretches of a playful grin start to appear. "I don't speak bullshit."

I playfully roll my eyes. "Sure you don't." I eye the splint he holds. "Why do you have that?"

Carson holds it out to me. "It's for you. I figure you could use it for your wrist."

"Why?" That's the response that I voice out. On the inside, I can feel my chest flutter slightly and my brain is running laps in my head trying to figure out why he's doing this.

"So it doesn't hurt anymore." He grabs my wrist and gently slips it on. The black brace is a little loose at first but he carefully pulls on the straps to tighten it. Not too much, but just enough. "Just slip it on when you're home and it flares up again and take it off when it gets better. It's pretty simple."

I just stare at him, like he's speaking a language I can't understand. Why is he doing this?

More important, did he just have that thing lying around his house?

That's really sweet of him, though. He's helping me with something so minuscule and normal to me that it renders me speechless.

Like anyone with a set of functioning brain cells, Carson notices my lack of response. "Did I do something wrong?"

I shake my head out of the daze I put myself in—literally and metaphorically—as I lightly graze the black splint that now dons my wrist. "Not at all," I manage to choke out.

I look back up to meet Carson's gaze and his eyes soften in relief. "Oh, thank fuck," he says in a low voice, which elicits a small yet quiet laugh out of me.

"Well, thanks," I say.

He shrugs. "It's no big deal." Carson steps back from the door. "I should head back. Sleep well." He waves and trots over to his front door.

I watch for a moment longer as the front door to his house closes and it's only then when I close the door of my own house and lean against it. Studying the splint wrapped around my arm, I allow a smile to escape for a second before Emma's words break into my thoughts.

"Are you sure he's just tutoring you?"

I head towards the kitchen, grab a napkin, ball it up, and—with my left hand—playfully throw it at Emma. It lightly touches her glossy black hair before floating to the ground. She laughs at my disappointing attempt.

"I'm just saying." Emma holds both hands up as if in surrender. "That looked a lot like something else."

I raise a brow at her statement. "Like what?"

Placing her hands back down to her keyboard, she continues typing away. But only replies with, "like he's crushing on you. Hard."

12

Field Trip, Yay!

Carson

Nobody will ever tell you this, but I love Halloween.

The one day a year where you can expect the unexpected frights and crazy costumes. It's mostly people in some variation of *Ghostface* or Michael Myers but still crazy, especially the weekend prior.

Halloweekend.

I'm sitting on the living room couch, watching Halloween (the first one, of course) when Mason and Jake rush down the stairs and towards the front door. Odd, it's still light out and we haven't talked about attending any parties.

"Where are you guys going?" I ask. Both boys freeze in their tracks and swivel around.

Mason slaps Jake's shoulder. "You couldn't run faster? And quieter?"

"Trying to keep up with black Barry Allen over here?" Jake scolds. "Fuck no, I couldn't. Maybe *you* should've *slowed down* for us short folk."

"Guys!" Their arguing is driving me insane.

Mason and Jake share a glance—or more of a glare, considering how annoyed they both look at each other—and eventually, it's Mason who responds. "We're going to Horror Nights with the girls."

I look at the window, where the sunlight glares at us, and turn back to them. "It's still day out."

Jake raises a brow. "Traffic."

"That would still take twenty minutes," I point out. "Anyway, why wasn't I invited?"

Mason lets out a laugh, which is a bit of a rarity. The guy is known for being the stoic, silent type. At least, in comparison to us. "We had this planned for a month now."

"Still—"

"And the birthday girl still hated your guts at the time so she didn't invite you," he finishes, and I freeze.

It's Diana's birthday? How did I not know this? Birthdays are always something to talk about in my opinion. For most people, it's the one day a year where everything is about them. I think back to every tutoring session we've had together.

Not a single session has she brought up her birthday.

Jake nods as if this isn't news to him. Of course, it fucking isn't. "Yeah, because Diana's birthday is on a weekday, we agreed to go this weekend. You know, when the park is at its scariest. And I wanted an excuse to visit Bailey while she's there."

I would pretend to gag at the mention of my cousin but I'm still surprised that Diana never said anything. Then again, I've learned over the past couple of weeks that she prefers to listen and observe than place herself in the spotlight.

"Ryder, can you hear me?" Jake waves a hand in front of my face and I swat it away. "I asked if she invited you."

"I didn't even know it was her birthday," I mumble. Shaking that thought away, I grab my wallet and house keys. "Would it be weird if I did?"

"I don't see a problem with it." Jake shrugs. "She doesn't hate you anymore now, does she?"

There's a question that I can't answer. Does she still hate me? At the most, I assume she tolerates me. I am helping her understand the obstacle course which is college calculus.

"Doesn't he need money for the tickets?" Mason points out so graciously.

"I have an annual pass." Family trips to Universal Studios are not uncommon for the Ryder family. Every year, during the Christmas season, we spend a week down in LA with my uncle, Bailey's dad. When Carly and I turned eighteen, he gave each of us individual passes.

It's crazy to me, but Carly and my cousin are not fazed by it whatsoever.

"Of course, he fucking does," Mason mutters, which gets a laugh out of me. "In that case, I'm fairly sure that Diana won't care."

With that knowledge in mind, I follow Mason and Jake outside to the front yard, where everyone else is congregating. Ronnie and Enzo are animatedly conversing about what to do and where to go.

"Guess who decided to crash the party!" Jake calls out.

"And guess who told me to?" I respond with the same volume, earning me a light shove on the shoulder.

Lucia turns away from the group and smiles when she sees me. "Thank goodness! We're at even numbers with you here, Carson."

"What's going on?" Mason asks as he approaches Lucia, wrapping an arm around her shoulder. I furrow my brows. That's a new development.

"They're trying to figure out the carpool situation."

"I thought it was between me and Ronnie," Jake says. "We're the only ones who have cars."

I step out of the conversation and towards the rest of the group. Emma is on her phone, Adrian is talking to Madi—again, a new development—and then there's Diana.

How can a girl steal all my attention by doing absolutely nothing? Except, well, fiddle with her thumbs. Diana's wrist is in a splint yet again. I feel somewhat accomplished that she took my advice and wore it when needed. She doesn't use it all the time but still...

She does look a little uncomfortable right now as everyone discusses the transportation situation.

I slowly approach her. "Not a single word, birthday girl?"

She turns to face me, almost surprised to see me there. "It's not crazy. Just a birthday."

"Just a birthday? Of course, it's crazy important! It's not every day someone turns twenty-one."

"Twenty," she corrects. "I'm turning twenty."

Oh. "I thought you were older."

She furrows her dark brows at me. "Should I take that as a compliment?"

I snort. "You have seen the guys I live with, right? Trust me when I say that it's the highest of compliments." Raising a brow, I ask, "So what grade did you skip?"

"No, I just graduated a year early," she explains.

"Wow. I feel like you should be tutoring me and not the way around."

"In calculus?" She laughs. "No thank you."

"Look at you guys getting along," Lucia chimes. "So which car are you guys going in?"

"I'm going with Jake," I answer immediately. Mainly because I'm the better driver of us two. Not to brag but it's true.

Diana shrugs. "What about everyone else?"

"Emma and Enzo are going with Ronnie," she answers. "To no one's surprise. Mason's joining them."

"So you're going with Ronnie, then?"

"Do you want me to go with you?" Lucia puts her hand on Diana's shoulder. "I can tell Mason that—"

"No, it's fine," Diana assures her. "Sit with Mason if you want to. Have fun cuddling with the big soft teddy bear."

The comparison is so absurd it makes me laugh. I press the palm of my hand onto my forehead. "Mason? A teddy bear? That's too good."

Lucia stares at me in confusion and it's then I choose to stop laughing. Okay, so they're both serious.

I clear my throat, facing Diana. "If Ronnie's car seats five people, then that means you're stuck with me and Jake."

"Fine with me." Although the tinge of red in her cheeks tells me otherwise.

"Come on." I gesture for Diana to follow me. We walk towards Jake's sedan—a dark gray Honda Civic—out by the driveway. Jake, Madi, and Adrian meet us there and Jake circles to the passenger's side, tossing me the keys.

I catch them in mid-air, thankful I popped a couple of Dramamine earlier today.

This evening just got interesting.

13

Driving Sucks

Diana

I hate cars.

Nothing spikes my heart rate more than sitting—or standing—in a moving vehicle. I've spent the past six years avoiding them whenever possible, and that's worked out somewhat well. But living in California means I don't have the option of walking there myself because of how large and stuffy the city is.

Los Angeles adds a whole new definition to the word *stuffy*.

The only thing keeping me sane at the moment is holding onto the handlebar with my left hand while my right wrist—which is currently in the splint Carson gave me—rests on my lap, right onto the dark gray seat belt.

Chase Atlantic's "Meddle About" playing from the car speakers would help keep my mind off of the fact that we're stuck on the freeway if Carson and Jake weren't arguing about the choice of music.

"You could have played anything else in the world," Carson argues. "Why this song?"

"Because I like it," Jake retorts back. "Remember the car rules? Passenger picks the music while the driver shut his piehole."

Madi chuckles next to me, while Adrian sighs. "They do this every time."

"Isn't this Jake's car?" I ask Adrian.

He nods.

"Then why is Carson driving?"

"I don't know," he tells me. "Jake and Carson were roommates before the rest of us came into the picture so for them, it's normal, I guess. I don't ask about it."

Not helpful, Adrian.

I move my eyes forward, to see what song is about to play when my eyes connect with Carson's blue ones in the rearview mirror. His eyes are softened, lines in between his brows that are somehow darker than the rest of his hair. Or maybe in comparison to his ivory-colored skin.

I glance away and look back down at my lap, fiddling with the fingers that are still exposed from the splint wrapped around my wrist.

Normally, when I'm in a situation that leaves me no other choice but to step inside a car, bus, or whatever fucking mode of transportation that exists, I focus on breathing carefully, and keep my ears tuned to a certain noise.

Since I didn't bring headphones, the noise would be the music playing. The music then gets overshadowed by Carson's laugh at something Jake said.

How did I go from barely tolerating Carson Ryder to noticing every minuscule detail about him? Like the guy is made out of some crazy aphrodisiac that I can't get enough of. Everyone has that. For me, it's the taste of my favorite cherry soda or sweet treat. Or Carson's cologne, apparently.

The guy always has this woodsy scent that follows him. I've only noticed because it's intense. No other reason, I swear.

"Diana." I blink and turn to find Madi's eyes on me. "Did you hear what I asked?"

I shake my head. "You asked for something?"

She eyes me in concern, brows dipping. "I asked if you were okay."

I shrug. "I'm fine. Just thinking about how scary Horror Nights in Hollywood will be."

Madi chuckles. "Probably nowhere near as crazy as Orlando."

"True." Around this time, every year, my family and I would make the three-hour long drive from Miami to Orlando to attend Horror Nights for my birthday. The last time we all attended was probably the best birthday I ever had.

Even seven years later, I still remember it.

"The actors were allowed to touch you in Orlando," I beam, thinking back to those birthdays. "Last time, a zombie accidentally stepped on Crystal's shoe and she screamed like a fucking banshee."

My little sister is still terrified of zombies to this day but I believe that to be a more reasonable fear—because at least they don't exist in real life.

"Can you imagine the *Friday the Thirteenth* walkthrough?" Madi's eyes light up. "That one's gonna be great."

I am so thankful that Madi is distracting me right now—even if she's clueless—because I was about one freeway exit away from fainting. Sounds dramatic but fainting in a tight space like this car is no joking matter.

Luckily, Carson exits the freeway and drives up the path that leads to the parking lot of Universal Studios. Once he parks and the engine finally dies, I practically rip the seatbelt off my person and jump out of the car faster than any speedster ever could.

Fresh air in Hollywood doesn't exist but it beats staying inside the car for so long.

Madi hops out right after me, checking her leggings and sweater before closing the door. She's wearing a pumpkin-themed sweater, a bright orange turtleneck with a classic jack-o-lantern face. "That was a fun ride," she smiles. Madi is a literal ball of sunshine.

How is she interested in Adrian of all people? Opposites really do attract, I guess.

"Yeah," I mutter, fidgeting with the strap of my splint. "Fun."

Jake approaches the two of us. "Ronnie and the others parked on the other lot so we're just going to meet them at the entrance."

We all start our trek towards the park entrance. I'm walking next to Madi, who is absentmindedly cracking her knuckles as she listens to Adrian gush about the studio tour tram that they "must ride first."

On second thought, I understand now.

A hand grasps my left shoulder and pulls me back. I almost turn around and smack the guy before noticing Carson's concerned eyes pinned on me yet again. "Are you okay?" He asks softly.

It doesn't take a genius to realize that he's talking about the car ride here.

Nodding, I lift his hand off my shoulder, which now feels cold from the absence. "I'm fine," I bite out.

Carson tilts his head, strands of dark hair falling to the side and a frown turning his lips. "Are you sure about that? You kind of looked like you were about to pass out, earlier. Or vomit. Maybe both."

"Well, I didn't," I tell him, my tone of voice annoyed. "I'm wide awake, with my stomach still inside my body." Usually, in the dying seconds after a mini-panic attack, I can get a little bitchy. I shouldn't take it out on him because Carson's genuinely concerned about me.

And the thought of that alone causes my stomach to bounce around a bit.

I take a deep breath and count to three, allowing my organs to catch up with each other. "Sorry. But thanks for the check-up, Doc."

He observes me for a little longer before nodding and I turn back around to catch up with Madi, who is listening intently to what Adrian has to say about...something. I don't know—I'm not paying much attention to him.

My attention was shot by the boy walking behind me.

14

No Rides, Just Sweet Stuff

Carson

Yeah, there's no way in hell I'm going on that.

All ten of us are standing right outside the *Revenge of the Mummy* indoor rollercoaster. The moment I saw the sign, I instantly took a step back from the rest of the group, which led to a lot of complaining.

From the guys, except for Jake, who doesn't care. He's probably the only one who knows why I'm not hesitant about avoiding the roller-coaster.

"Carson, it's in the dark!" Enzo's been trying to persuade me to go on with them from the beginning. "You won't be able to see the mummies or anything."

"There's still the bugs," Emma points out.

"That's not what I'm worried about," I say. Indoor rollercoasters in the dark are still rollercoasters, and I draw the line at them.

"Well, I'm going on," Jake tells the rest of the group. "Anyone else joining?"

Everyone hums in agreement, except for Diana. Her head's tilted slightly downwards at her boots and for the second time today, she looks a little pale. Her beautifully tanned skin went about five shades lighter and is about as pale as I am.

Okay, she's still tan but metaphorically speaking, she's as white as the bandages that are probably on the animatronic mummies I don't ever plan on viewing.

Diana and I stay in place while the others head in line for the mummy rollercoaster. This is the second time we've been left alone together, separated from each of our respective friend groups, and of our own

68

choice. The circumstances were different last time but now? She chose not to stay with the group.

But with me.

After a minute of awkward silence that sits between us, Diana finally speaks up. "Why didn't you go with them?"

I shrug. "I'm not good with rollercoasters," I answer and leave it at that. The real reason behind that is so damn embarrassing that only Jake knows.

"Me neither," she says meekly. "So, what do we do know?"

I swivel my head around the area. I've visited this park so often in the past twenty years that I should know the entire place with the back of my hand. Somehow, I come up empty.

"I'm at a loss," I admit to her. "What do you want to do, birthday girl?"

"I don't know. It's my first time here."

My jaw drops slightly. "You've never been here? But you've lived in LA for a couple of years, now."

"Not to this location," she explains hastily. "The Orlando location is a lot different."

"Right." She did bring that up in the car ride over.

"Also, can we just not make my birthday a big deal right now?" She suggests. "It's just a hang out with all eight of our roommates."

I shake my head, holding back a laugh as we walk farther away from the rollercoaster and toward the center of the lower lot. "I can't. Diana, this is the one day a year where everything is literally about you. Wait, when is your actual birthday?"

She mumbles something I can't understand.

"Can you repeat that?"

The mumbles are a little louder but still incoherent.

"Diana—"

"It's on Thursday!" She finally blurts out and I now understand why.

"But that's Halloween," I point out.

She sighs. "No kidding. I hate having it on a major holiday."

"Me too," I mutter.

Diana furrows her brows in curiosity and I find myself explaining. "Carly and I were born on July Fourth."

"That sucks."

"We're used to it." Gesturing around us, I announce, "Well, the park is your limit. And I'm just here for the food and overly-sweet stuff."

At the mention of sweets, her pretty eyes light up. "Speaking of sweet stuff, where's Hogsmeade?"

3 . 1 4 1 5 9 2 6 5 3 5 9

Twenty minutes, two long escalator rides, and a split churro later, we arrive in the Harry Potter section of the park. I've only seen the movies but I can tell—based on the bright smile on Diana's face—that she's a bigger Potterhead than my cousin Bailey ever was.

"This is just as magical as I remember," she marvels as she glances between the two buildings in front of us while we wait in line for but-terbeer. "I just wish I brought my robes with me."

"Robes?"

She nods. "My Hufflepuff robes."

My jaw drops yet again. It doesn't surprise me that she has Harry Potter robes—that girl goes all out for the things she cares about—but Diana being a Hufflepuff was not on my Diana Blanco Bingo card. "You? A Hufflepuff?"

She snorts after glancing at the shocked expression on my face. "Why are you so surprised? You've seen my pajamas."

I hold my hands up. "I thought they were hand-me-downs."

"Well they weren't," she confirms. "I took that test a long time ago and I was such a different person back then."

"No kidding."

"Well, what's your house?" She asks.

I shrug. "Never took the quiz. Maybe I'm a Ravenclaw." Finally, we reach the front of the line and order two for each of us. I get the hot version, while Diana orders the frozen ButterBeer—which is just a but-terscotch slushy with white foam on top.

"That's just crazy to me," she declares as she fishes in her bag for her wallet. "First, you don't know what Hogwarts house you're in and now you're trying to pay for my ButterBeer."

I place my hand over her bag. "I've got it."

"No, Carson. I was the one who suggested we get some so it's only fair if I pay for it."

"It's your birthday, so I insist."

"So do I," she says, looking up from her bag to face me. "Trust me, doc. You've already done more than enough for me. So the least I can do is pay for your drink. So Carson, whatever your middle name is, Ryder, let me pay!"

My heartbeat quickens its pace and I'm pretty sure people can hear it from inside the Wands attraction near us.

That's a first for me.

I can't say that someone has insisted on paying for or doing anything for me in the past. I can't recall a time when that's happened. So never expecting anything in return was my normal. If I didn't know any better, I would have expected Diana to just give in and let me pay but prior experience has taught me that she can be stubborn when she wants to be.

But if her stubbornness means pushing her attention towards me? Doing something for me?

"Are you sure?" I ask.

She pulls out her wallet, curtain bangs falling in her eyes. After grabbing a card and handing it to the vendor—who I now realize has been listening to this conversation, the nosy fucker—she responds without a hint of hesitation in her voice. "Why wouldn't I be?"

This girl might just be the death of me and it's an ending I'm just waiting for.

15

NOT Bartholomew

Diana

If you told me two months ago that I would enjoy being around Carson Ryder, I would have laughed in your face.

Because, as some may have it, he's easy to talk to. Even outside our tutoring sessions, in the middle of the upper lot of Universal Studios, I'm having a fucking blast with just the two of us.

Since it's Saturday, and the park is very crowded, we've resorted to resting by one of the auditoriums where they used to hold the special effects show, just asking each other random questions.

Through it, I did get to learn his middle name and he learned mine—it's Jameson—our conversation has shifted mainly towards me because he wants to know what the park in Orlando is like.

"So she went up to hug the guy? Was your sister not aware of the fake blood?" Carson is still shocked at my little sister's lack of spatial awareness.

I shrug. "If you were my sister, you wouldn't notice." Even now, I think Crystal's spatial awareness has gotten worse than it was when she was eight.

"Shouldn't we be waiting for the others to get off the ride?" I suggest at the exact moment my phone buzzes in my bag. I pull it out to find a text from Ronnie waiting.

Ronnie

> We're going on the ride next door so you and Carson should eat without us.

I chuckle softly. Leave it to the adrenaline junkie to wait another hour in line for his thrill. "Let's go," I tell Carson, shoving my phone back into my bag.

"Was that Adrian texting you?" He furrows his brows.

"Ronnie," I reply.

He scoffs as we make our way over to the carnival games. "Leave it to the two adrenaline junkies. You'd think Adrian would have enjoyed this show over the rides but if he's not falling to his death, then it's not worth it."

"Are you just being dramatic?"

"Those were words out of Adrian's mouth."

"He might have a point," I say. "The one in Orlando looked boring."

He places a hand over his chest. "Wow, Diana. You wound me."

"What? Was the show actually interesting?"

"Like no other," he clarifies, a little glint in his eyes. Probably from thinking back to a good memory. "They filmed multiple shows and movies in this park. My family and I got to volunteer for a demonstration when I was nine. We all got to wear those suits with the green balls on them."

That does sound a little cool. I, however, would have been frightened by the prospect of standing up in front of people. Kudos to little Carson for having that confidence. Because at that age? I would have cowered. Even now, I would have cowered if I had been thrust into the spotlight like that.

"What do you say?" We stop at a ring toss game, where the prizes are all related to one of the animated movies displayed in the section of the park we're in. The yellow and purple minions and those huge unicorns are all they have.

But I know better. "Those games are a sham."

Carson makes a face. "The claw machines are scams. These aren't." He motions to the ring toss.

"Have you ever won a prize from them?"

"I haven't. But they look so easy."

"Oh, you sweet summer child," I sigh. "That's what they want you to think." I have yet to see one of the game attendants pull a stuffed minion from the shelves and a kid walking away happy with it.

"Then I'm going to prove you wrong," he declares, chin up high.

Both of my brows fly up my face. "You are going to attempt this game?"

He slams a five-dollar bill on the table. "Correction, I am going to *win* it." The attendant rests a set of five rings on the table in front of us. Carson grabs the bright orange ring on top and focuses on the bottles inside the booth. "No doubt about it."

I attempt to cross my arms over my waist, but the splint makes the motion uncomfortable so I keep my arms to my sides. "Well, may Fortuna be upon you."

He raises a brow. "You mean *fortune*."

"I know what I said," I mumble.

I'm a little glad he didn't ask me to help because my aim is complete garbage. Maybe that's why I think these games are a hoax—because I can't win a single one of them.

He tosses the first two rings and both of them bounce off the rims of the bottles and onto the floor.

I wince. "Bummer."

"I've got three left, D," he reminds me, eyes still on the game. Without looking down, he grabs a ring and tosses it without a second thought. We watch it fall around the neck of the bottle and onto the table, surrounding the base of the metal bottle.

Ay, mierda. My jaw drops and stays that way when he does it again with his remaining rings.

"Pick your prize from the middle two rows," the game attendant tells Carson in the most monotone voice I've ever heard—and I thought the priest at my mom's funeral was duller than a sack of unwashed potatoes.

Carson places one finger on his chin, concentrating deeply. "What do you think I should pick, Diana?"

"How?" I'm still shocked that he won and yet he's all nonchalant about it.

He shrugs, smirking. "I just have good aim."

Not even Apollo has that great of aim, and he's the god of archery.

I stare amongst the vast three choices presented. "I don't know. They all look the same."

"Really?"

"Not literally," I say. "But it's not like you need to feel connected to a certain one."

"True," he agrees. "But what about the one *you* feel connected to?"

I laugh softly. "It's not like you're gonna give it to me."

He doesn't say another word. I turn to face his side profile (of course, his side profile is handsome) and my heart starts beating faster than normal. Was he going to?

I switch my focus to the prizes, my eyes stopping at a particular, tall yellow minion. "Maybe that one." I point to it.

He points to the yellow one-eyed guy and the attendant removes him from the shelves and hands it to Carson. "Congratulations," says the robot attendant.

"I got to say," Carson begins as we walk away from the booth. "This guy is a lot bigger than he looked on the shelves."

The stuffed minion in question is so big that it reaches just below Carson's chin. He's holding the stuffed minion by the waist and for some reason, I find myself wishing I was in that minion's place.

I am not someone who gets jealous so easily, especially where a stuffed minion that speaks incoherently and eats nothing but bananas is concerned.

"What's this minion's name again? I can never remember."

He shrugs. "He looks like a Steve."

"Steve?" I shake my head. "No, that's too basic."

"What were you going to suggest? Carl?"

We continue to go back and forth with names. Once I suggested Donald, another time, he picks Bartholomew and it's then we realize that not only naming the minion is a lost cause, but that Carson sucks at picking names.

I decided right there that if I ever have children, I'm not going to Carson for help naming them.

All the walking around gets the both of us hungry so we stop at a restaurant for dinner. It's been too long and I'm willing to bet that the rest of our friends are still waiting in line for a water ride, or whatever ride it was they chose to wait in line for.

"Can we just alternate this time?" Carson suggests when we reach the front of the line. "You paid for butterbeer, so I should pay for lunch."

I shake my head. "You paid for Trent!"

"We're not naming the minion Trent!" He laughs. "Besides, he doesn't count."

Since I'm the one holding onto the minion, I squeeze it tightly in my arms. "You just hurt his feelings."

"I'm only counting anything we can eat." He points to the minion. "We're not eating William."

"We're not naming the minion William, either," I say before sighing. "I guess if you're only counting food, then fine. You can pay."

"Thank you." He pays and we take our trays over to a table that just cleared up. I place my tray down and sit the stuffed minion on the chair next to me before I perch myself on the cold, metal chair. We start eating and not much is said between us. I normally don't mind it because I'm rather used to it but with my average-tasting tacos from the Mexican restaurant, I'd rather have something or someone to distract me.

It's not much longer before I find myself unable to finish my food. Maybe I'm just used to the taco trucks near my house or amusement park food is so not worth the price (I'm going with the latter here). There's also the possibility that my mind is still on the boy in front of me, eating his loaded nachos without care.

For once.

"Hey, you okay?" Carson's muffled voice asks as he wipes his mouth with a napkin.

I blink and nod. "Yeah," I lie. "Just a little worried about Friday's test." Due to the multiple people who did horribly on the mid-term, our professor is issuing a re-do midterm. Something he should have done because, since the original test, there hadn't gone a day that a student *wasn't* begging for one. We got to a point where Lucia started a petition just for it.

Carson softly smiles at me and reaches over to touch my hand. Well, he touches the splint but I can still feel him regardless. "You'll do fine."

"But what if I fail?" I whine.

"Please," he says. "You've been doing great in our sessions so far. Understood the material quickly. It's never been a *you* problem. You'll pass."

I shake my head. "Do you really believe in me?"

"Well, yeah." He shrugs. "I'll always believe in you, D."

Oh great, my face is burning up and it has nothing to do with the tacos I ate. Why do so few words have to affect me so greatly?

"Well, you were easy to understand," I admit, attempting another bite at my tacos before pushing the plate away. "Ugh, I can't do this anymore."

He pulls the plate closer to him and takes a bite of an untouched taco. After a few chews, his face scrunches up. "Yeah, that sucks," he agrees after swallowing the bite. "Maybe it's the cilantro."

"It's never the cilantro." I wrap an arm around the stuffed minion. "At least Anthony didn't get to eat it. The lucky guy."

"We're not naming him Anthony!"

"Well, it's better than Bartholomew," I laugh, remembering his first suggestion.

He exhales, allowing his bangs to fly away from his face. "Then you can call him Barty if that's better."

"You are going to die on this Bartholomew hill, aren't you?"

Carson laughs and it doesn't sound fake or diluted. It's a whole-hearted, genuine laugh that I don't remember ever hearing before this moment.

He has me laughing alongside him and as we're enjoying this moment between us, I realize how much I want this to keep going.

How I don't want any of this to end.

"So, if you weren't having the time of your life with the coolest guy on the planet"—he winks—"what would you spend your birthday doing?"

I playfully roll my eyes. "Honestly?"

He shrugs. "What other way would you answer?"

"I could lie to your face and you wouldn't know," I hum. "But I won't. Honestly, I would be eating a lot of cherries."

Carson arches a brow. "Cherries?"

I smile nervously. "My mom and I were obsessed with cherry-flavored anything and since our birthdays were close to each other, we would buy up half the cherry supply at Publix and watch our favorite movies." She would joke that we kept all the cherry harvesters in business.

"She sounds fun," he muses.

I nod, trying to keep my composure because talking about my mom makes me a little too emotional for public display. "She was," I mumble, mostly to myself.

Carson takes the hint and drops the brief subject of my mother. "Cherry-everything, though? Isn't that a lot?"

"Hey," I chastise. "Don't knock it until you try it." To get a rise out of Carson, I take a piece of loose cilantro from the taco—the only good thing about it if you ask me—and pop it into my mouth like I would with popcorn.

"Never mind."

I lift my chin in victory.

16

Sweet Suffering Lips

Carson

"Why?" Enzo and Ronnie approach me by the first—and largest—maze entrance. "Just why?" Enzo repeats his question, eyes stuck on the minion in my arms.

Diana's arm got a little sore after holding onto Bartholomew (yes, I'm sticking with the name) for a while so I offered to keep an eye on him while giving her arms a break.

"Why not?" I counter with. "I won it fair and square."

"It's pretty funny. You look like a proud dad," Ronnie adds. "What did Diana name it?"

I smile proudly. "His name is Bartholomew."

"No! I didn't pick that!" Diana shouts, causing the two guys in front of me to burst out laughing.

"You know," Ronnie quips. "I genuinely thought you wouldn't make it out of those tutoring sessions alive. Guess I was wrong."

"All of your limbs are intact," Enzo points out cheerfully.

I narrow my eyes at the happy couple, squeezing the minion in my arms. "Very funny, guys."

Ronnie shrugs. "I thought it was. Anyway, are you going to enter the maze?"

I look up at the entrance in front of me. Maybe I'm going crazy but I swear I can hear lightning and it's not even raining. My list of fears does not consist of the superficial, common childhood frights—zombies, werewolves, clowns—but that maze looks like the beginning of the end.

And not the *Stairway to Heaven* kind of end. Like every still of *The Walking Dead* and *The Last of Us* combined into one, megamind obstacle course.

"I might," is the response I settle with. "Maybe not alone."

"Well, you're not going with us." Enzo backs up and since he's holding onto Ronnie's hand, his boyfriend follows.

What happened between the time Diana and I left them and when we met up hours later for Horror Nights?

Just as my mind would have it, my head swivels behind me, where Diana and her roommates were. Past tense because now they don't occupy that space.

Dammit. There goes my chance to ask her.

It's not like she would have said yes anyway. We spent almost the entire afternoon together and some of the evening. It would be a miracle if she wasn't already tired of me now.

"I'm going to the Texas Chainsaw Massacre maze," Enzo announces. "It doesn't look as terrifying."

As they scramble away from the entrance of the maze, I allow myself to laugh at their cowardice—the wimps.

Looks like you're on your own this time, Ryder.

I take a deep breath and approach the front of the line, where a girl with the standard park employee uniform waits. "How many?"

"Just me," I answer, to which she shakes her head and clicks her tongue.

"Bad choice, my dude. Good luck."

The unspoken rule: never walk into a haunted maze alone. I step inside the maze and am instantly, greeted by a scare actor, in full makeup and costume, popping out of the left wall. I raise my brows at him and continue walking.

This might be hard to believe, but tonight's adventure is my first foray into Halloween Horror Nights. Sure, I have an annual pass but with college, work, and the distance—I grew up in Silicon Valley, which is at least a ten-hour drive from here—my family and I never got the chance.

My uncle was the one who gifted me and my sister the passes. Not my parents and I can't thank him enough because I was the twin who enjoyed this park—not Carly, which is kind of ironic.

After turning a corner, another zombie pops out and I jump. Okay, that was a good scare. This zombie, in particular, is a short girl around my age with extremely tattered blonde hair.

I wave with my free hand. "Hi, Bailey."

She doesn't say anything. Of course, she can't. As a scare actor, she's not allowed to break character. I wonder how far Jake got because he knew this was the maze Bailey was working.

For the most part, it takes two more scare actors to jump before I give up and turn around and start going back the way I came. Maybe this maze isn't for me. It looked hella scary on the outside but—except for my cousin—it's a disappointment within.

That description hits a little too close to home.

Before I can turn another corner, I feel something tough bump into Bartholomew, who is practically pinned to my chest.

"Oof! *Mierda*!"

I tense slightly because I only know one person who habitually curses in Spanish, and it's sure as hell, not Jake—and he's a Spanish major.

I press both of my hands on Diana's shoulders, effectively dropping the stuffed minion, and steadying her. When I look up from her, I realize that she's not alone. Two of her roommates—Madi and Emma, to be more specific—accompany her.

Madi is the first one to speak. "Hey, Carson. Is it just you?"

I nod.

"Is this maze somewhat scary? This one over here got bored during the *Friday the Thirteenth* walkthrough." She jabs a thumb at Diana, who turns redder than the ribbon in her hair.

"Jason Voorhees was not as scary as in the movie," she murmurs, picking up Bartholomew from the ground. "It was disappointing."

"Well, I hate to break it to you girls," I say. "But so is this one. I was just about to leave."

Emma sighs in relief. "Thank goodness." Then, her eyes widen. "Not to you leaving, but the scare."

"Emma's a little jumpy," Diana explains. "The zombies aren't that horrifying."

"So you say," Emma says sarcastically.

I check my watch for the time. The night is still young and I don't plan on visiting every attraction in Horror Nights. Only the ones that are worth it.

"I'll keep you girls company," I suggest. "Ward off all the scary zombies."

Madi hums, Emma nods, while Diana sarcastically responds with, "Our hero."

I turn back around and, once again, start walking through the not-a-maze maze, while the other girls follow. I see the same two scare actors that made me want to leave and Diana quickens her pace so that she stands right by my side.

"I must say, watching you win that minion was far more interesting than this." She gestures to the walls around us.

I huff. "No kidding. And you did this every year for your birthday?"

"Mostly the park rides," she clarifies. "I don't get scared easily but Florida knows how to scare people."

No kidding. I've only been to Florida one time but everyone knows that state to be the crazy one. Forget the Sunshine State, it's the birth spot of all unimaginable monsters—I mean Florida men.

Diana starts giggling, and it's only then I realize that I said all of that out loud. Someone kill me, please. Particularly the zombies in this maze.

"You're not wrong—" She begins to say when Emma lets out a scream so guttural it has both of our heads turning.

Another zombie popped out and she's cocooned inside of Madi's arms, trembling. Madi's mouth is moving but I don't know what she's saying.

"Is she okay?" Diana asks, worried.

Madi nods. "We just might turn around and head back from where we came."

"We'll go with you."

She waves a hand. "Nonsense. We'll be fine. You two finish the journey." The two girls start to walk off, leaving me and Diana with Bartholomew in her arms. The minion is so big it almost shields Diana entirely.

"Did she just leave us here?" Diana wonders out loud as we continue walking. "Again? In the middle of the most boring maze. Traitor."

"Would you rather be stuck here alone?" I grill.

She opens her mouth to say something but what follows instead is a small scream when two scare actors jump from behind her. Diana drops Bartholomew and reaches for my arm, pulling herself closer to me. Her back to my chest and I instinctively squeeze her tighter, inhaling her scent.

Cherries. Of course, she smells sweet, like cherries.

"You know what," Diana says shakily. "I take back my previous statement. This isn't boring at all."

Agreed. Seeing Diana scared had me scared for a minute. My head bends down slightly to find Diana's wide eyes on me. Her breathing is a little shaky, but her cherry-red lips are what catch my attention.

Right in front of me.

Just an inch closer...

Screams disrupt my thoughts and the moment, causing Diana and me to jump away from each other as if cactus pricks were stuck to our clothes. I allow my heartbeat to slow down and mentally count to three in my head before glancing behind me. Footsteps approach and with each one, I can hear voices.

Great. A whole group of people just ruined the moment.

Diana looks back up at me and jabs a thumb at the trail in front of us. "We should probably keep going."

Running one hand through my hair, I nod, picking up Bartholomew. "Yeah."

I follow her the rest of the way and the zombies don't even faze me. My mind doesn't keep track of the going-ons of the maze. It sticks to the memory that happened only a moment ago.

I almost kissed Diana in the middle of the maze. And if it weren't for the family walking towards us, I would have.

17

The Feelings Are Back Again
Diana

Happy birthday to me, right?

I immediately open the door of my house and get greeted with a bunch of confetti cannons. I've been dozing off in my Legacy of Rome class today so this was definitely the wake-up call that I needed.

Still would have preferred a birthday Cubano.

"Happy birthday!" Ronnie cheers, blowing a birthday horn and dancing in place.

I laugh at his celebratory dance. "Thanks, Ronnie." I place my backpack down on the couch before heading towards the kitchen and straight for the moka pot. It may only be two in the afternoon but I only got three hours of sleep. Add that to the two-hour lecture on the literal Roman empire and I'm just about five steps closer to sleeping my birthday away.

But tomorrow is the re-do midterm for calculus, and I need to stay awake so I can finish studying. With Carson.

Ugh, the only reason I haven't been sleeping much is because of him. My damn mind has been keeping me awake with the memories of Saturday night at the maze. How close his lips were to mine. The way he kept me in his arms.

How neither of us wanted to let go.

Was that all in my head? I hope not.

I fill the moka pot insert with coffee grounds and the bottom half with water before setting it on the stove. Now I can wait, knowing that I won't be as grumpy as my usual morning self in about ten minutes. The sad thing about that is I'm usually an early riser. It must be the lack of sleep finally catching up to me.

"So." Ronnie approaches the kitchen fridge and grabs a diet soda can. "What are the birthday girl's plans?"

"We already celebrated my birthday," I remind him. "Remember?"

"Yeah, but today is the actual day. It's not every day a bad bitch turns twenty."

I snort at Ronnie's "bad bitch" comment. His enthusiasm knows no bounds. If I choose to make a birthday post, that will definitely be my caption. "Studying for a big test with Carson."

He sticks his tongue out. "You're no fun." After closing the refrigerator door, he saunters off, heading upstairs. "Have fun with lover boy!"

My face heats up. "Ronnie!"

A few minutes later, the coffee is ready, and after adding oat milk and ice, I carry the mug and my book bag upstairs to my room. Since I have today off from work and only one class to attend—my other class got canceled—I have mostly a free day that will be spent studying and continuing my *Gilmore Girls* marathon.

I place my headphones in my ears and begin looking over my notes. I don't know how much time has passed before someone knocks on my bedroom door. Looking up from the textbook, I find Carson munching on a bag of spicy chips and my eyes immediately drift to his lips before my brain can stop them.

"You ready?"

My eyes finally meet his blue ones and I nod. He places his bag on the floor and sits down right across from me. Full-on, criss-cross like I would do as a kid. It's a little adorable.

He holds out the bag of chips for me and after taking a couple of them, we return to studying. He quizzes me on theories from time to time and I answer the problems in the textbook that I haven't already. Lucia joins us after coming back, and the three of us make progress. Though, I know Carson isn't retaking the midterm since he doesn't need to—the lucky one—he doesn't need to be here helping us study.

But I'm thankful for it all the same.

When we finish, Carson waves goodbye to Lucia and me before heading out of my room and back downstairs, probably leaving the house overall. I close my book, let out a sigh, and pray that the re-do midterm will be a breeze.

Another nagging thought does sneak up to the forefront of my mind, however: Carson didn't wish me happy birthday. Not that I expected him to. But for a guy who claims to have an eidetic memory, I would have thought he would. It... hurts, a little.

Maybe what had happened in the maze was all in my head.

Lucia flops herself down onto her side of the room and groans. "This will be the death of me."

"Same," I agree.

She lifts her head off her silk pillow. "So, how's your birthday? Did you enjoy the box in the kitchen or something?

My ears perk up. "What box?" I didn't see a box.

"The white box on the kitchen counter, duh," she says. "The one with all the cherry-flavored Jolly Ranchers, lollipops, cherry cola that Ronnie had to put in the—"

I dash out of my room and down the stairs like a kid on Christmas—on Halloween, ironically—to see if Lucia is bluffing. Sure enough, she wasn't. There is a lot of cherry-flavored stuff.

Everything Lucia mentioned and more. "Oh my gosh," I whisper to myself.

After approaching the table, I pick up a cherry jolly rancher and pop it into my mouth before opening the box. Inside it sits the same cherry pie that Carson brought me before offering to tutor me, and a bright red envelope.

I reach for the envelope and open it up to find a card with his handwriting.

Did you really think I would forget your birthday? Think again. You may not be able to celebrate with your mom this year but I hope this is close enough. Happy birthday, Just Diana. - Carson

My heart swells up at the card. Carson did all of this? It must have taken him forever to pick out the cherry-flavored candies.

I can feel the happy tears coming up, and it's only then I realize: that maybe I am starting to fall for Carson. And not only does this excite me...

It terrifies me.

THE PI(E) TRUCE

3 . 1 4 1 5 9 2 6 5 3 5 9

Lucia and I sit with bated breath at our desks as Professor Scott passes out the midterm. Sweet Apollo of the burning chariot, it's starting to get hot here. Is it just me? I look around the classroom, at the students sitting at tables near and far. They're nervous too, right?

My eyes wander to the table behind me, where Carson would normally sit. The chair has been vacant since I arrived. But that's only because he's not needed in class today.

Lucky son-of-a-bitch.

Taking a deep breath, I pull out a pencil and my calculator and wait patiently for Scott to hand me my doom—I mean test.

Athena, please give me strength.

Eventually, he places the test face down on my table and I flip it over so I can begin. I scan each question before diving right into the first one. Surprisingly, I know what to do, unlike the last time I took the midterm.

It still takes me a while to finish up but I manage and once I place the test on Professor Scott's desk, my heart finally stops pounding in my head. I can breathe easier, knowing that I didn't have as much difficulty as I did last time.

That's a good sign, right?

I walk out of the classroom hurriedly because I'm running a little late for my shift. Even though Lottie knows about my re-do midterm, I don't want to take advantage of it by being late.

Something touches my shoulder, startling me just for a minute before I turn around and come face to face with a tall figure in a faded yet dark leather jacket.

At first, I'm worried, but I then find that all-too-familiar smile and kind eyes, and just about every tense muscle in my body loosens up.

Wait, what? "What are you doing here?" I ask Carson, confusion lacing my face.

He shrugs. "Just wanted to check on how you did."

"On your day off?"

87

He nods.

Wow. Okay. Not to downplay it, but did he not have anything better to do than check on his pupil?

"No other reason?"

"Well, how did you do?" He asks while walking alongside me.

I take a deep breath. "I think I did well. Definitely better than the last time."

Carson pats my shoulder and rubs it gently. "There we go!"

"That doesn't mean that I passed," I remind him. "Who knows? Maybe he'll see my work and fail me on the spot." And then my scholarship will disappear. Poof. Gone.

He shakes his head at the thought of me failing. "Yeah, I don't think that will happen. At all."

"It could."

"Diana." He stops me and places both hands on my shoulders, pinning me with his blue gaze. "You're going to pass. There isn't a damn bone in my body that believes otherwise because you are one of the smartest people I know and you worked hard for this, D."

"You helped," I remind him.

"I didn't take the test."

I hold back an eye-roll, laughing. "Shut up and take the credit, Carson."

He holds both hands up in surrender. "Fine, I'm taking the credit." When he finally laughs, it's like jingle bells rigging. A pleasant sound I didn't expect.

Yeah, I'm totally crushing.

18

I Might Have a Problem

Carson

On Wednesday morning, I drag myself into calculus. Even though it's only November and not that early, I still feel weary, like a ton of bricks hit me in the face, and I'm waking up from a coma.

The one thing that's making today more bearable is seeing Diana in the front two seats. Only today, she's alone. Usually, Lucia sits right next to her but today, she's not there.

I approach Diana's desk, tapping once to get her attention. She glances up, hazel-green eyes no longer shooting daggers at me. When that stopped, I'm not exactly sure.

"Well, you're chipper," I muse.

She shakes her head wildly. "Nope, it's all nerves."

"Why? It's just Wednesday."

"He's passing out the scores for the re-do midterm today," she corrects, fiddling with the strap on her splint. "That's why."

"You nervous?" I ask.

She shakes her head. "I feel just great, doc. Thanks." I can hear the sarcasm lacing her voice.

"Okay, class. Get your textbooks out," Professor Scott announces as he waltzes into the class. Really, he hobbles. His posture and stance are so bad that I'm pretty sure my great-uncle Carl can walk better than my sixty-something calculus professor.

I bet he can teach better than Scott.

But if that were the case, I wouldn't have had to tutor Diana these past few weeks and break through that icy persona that she only showcased when I was around—partially due to the pie I accidentally threw at her face—and unveil a lot more.

And I'm grateful for my professor's shitty teaching methods.

Nodding to the empty chair next to Diana, I ask. "Is this seat taken?"

She gestures for me to sit down, and I do so, grabbing my textbook and placing one headphone in. I wasn't lying to Diana when I told her that I didn't listen to his lectures. At least, not in their entirety. I jot notes down from time to time but for the most part, I spend the time I have in class answering the practice questions on the back of the textbook that I don't think the rest of our class knows about.

Hozier playing in one ear, Professor Scott droning on and on in the other. I, Carson Ryder, the multi-tasker the world never knew it needed.

About halfway through the lecture, he pauses and allows us five minutes of reprieve so he can pass out the scores for the re-do midterm. I quickly finish the question I'm working on and close my notebook before turning to Diana, who bounces her jean-clad knee in anticipation.

And at such a rapid pace that she repeatedly hits the desk lightly from underneath. I thought the knocking was coming from the music—I guess I was wrong.

I lift my hand from my desk and place it on her knee, causing her to turn to me with wide, confused eyes. "You'll be fine," I whisper, bringing my eyes back to my notebook.

After giving her knee one light squeeze, her shoulders loosen slightly, and I can feel that her knee has stopped bouncing. I don't blame her for being nervous. There's so much on the line for her with that midterm score.

Diana's name gets called. She stands up and pushes her chair before shaking her left wrist and heading over to his desk in the front of the classroom. When she finally reaches it, I tear my head away from the sight and try my utter fucking best to focus on just about *anything else*.

I'm already nervous *for* her.

She passed the re-do. I don't doubt that. So why do I feel nervous?

After what feels like forever, Diana finally approaches our desk and sits down quietly. This time, her eyes are wide and her face is as red as her lips, which are pressed together as if she's trying to contain herself.

"How did you do?"

Before she can answer, Scott resumes the lecture. Dammit, why couldn't he wait a little longer?

She leans closer to me. "After class," she whispers before focusing her attention back to the front of the class.

I don't think the clock ticked slower than in this lecture.

By the time class comes to an end, I stand right outside the classroom, waiting for Diana to follow. I add my second earphone in, music in full blast, any surrounding sounds muted by the guitar strings.

I'm not sure how much time has passed, but in the next instant, I am nearly tackled to the wall by a pair of thin arms and a body. Removing both headphones and re-adjusting to my surroundings, I then see Diana in an attempt to hug me.

That catches me by surprise. I never thought of her as a hugger—or one whose love language is physical touch—but I'm not complaining.

"Thank you, thank you," she repeats, squeezing me tighter. "Thank you."

My arms wrap around her frame and pull her closer, soaking in this very moment. I don't think a hug like this will be a daily occurrence for me, especially a hug from her.

"So, it's good news?"

She pulls back with eyes brighter than the lights in the building. "Carson, I got a ninety."

My eyes widen. "Wow, that's crazy."

Diana giggles. Wow, that girl just about never giggles, so it's a surprise to hear it. This girl is just full of delightful surprises, isn't she?

"I know, right? Granted, it's not as high as what you got the first time, but this will save my grade, Carson. Thank you. I owe you big time."

I shake my head in response. "No, you don't owe me anything."

"Like hell, I don't," she protests. "I will pay you back for this in some way."

"D, you don't need to—" I begin to say before she stops me.

"It's one thing to pay for butterbeer but that's all I've done." She places one hand on her hip. "You really don't know how to be selfish, do you?"

My brain comes to a screeching halt at the question. I'm not sure Diana was serious about it but that question hit me like a ton of bricks.

I know how to be selfish, right? I've been selfish multiple times in my life. Like how I'm always the designated driver, regardless. But then again, it puts the stress off anyone else who—

My fingers clench. Holy fuck, she might be right.

She then mutters something about running late for work, grabs her book bag from the floor, and meekly smiles at me before turning away, and briskly walking off, leaving me standing by the door without a word.

"What just happened over here?" Bailey asks as she appears right next to me.

I blink and turn to my cousin. "Geez, give a guy notice, why don't you?"

She rolls her eyes at me. "Whatever, man. Since when were you seeing someone? I didn't think that was possible."

"I'm not seeing anyone," I correct her. Though, as I stare off in the direction of the library, I wish that was a lie.

Bailey doesn't need to say anything but that gleam in her eyes speaks many words. Five of them being: I'm in real fucking deep.

19

A Distraction I Didn't Think I Needed

Diana

Did I just really tell someone that they don't know how to be selfish?

That's one of two things that are keeping me awake on a Sunday morning. In fact, it's so early that the damn sun is barely out. I actually did fall asleep but I had a recurring dream where I asked that question—which ended up with a completely different outcome—and it kept on waking me up because of some stupid explosion.

You know how dreams are.

The second reason? Because I need to video-call my family. It's only seven in the morning in Miami and both my sister and Dad do not believe in sleeping in. Especially on today of all days. I'm sad that I can't be over there today but the call is the closest I can get.

After tossing and turning for what feels like an eternity, I feel awake enough to move and slip out of bed. I quietly tiptoe around the darkness of my and Lucia's bedroom, being careful not to wake her up, and grab my cell phone, black robe, and fuzzy slippers as quietly as I can to not wake Lucia up.

Once I descend the stairs—like the graceful quiet fairy that I am *not*—I head for the back door and right outside the backyard.

Since moving to college, I have always made sure to wake up as early as possible before class or work to call my family on this day. Every year without fail. Thankfully, it's Sunday—a day in which I have neither. I still need to wake up due to the stupid three-hour time difference between here and Miami.

After taking a seat by one of the lawn chairs outside, I press the call button on Crystal's contact and wait for her to answer. It's no surprise that she answers after three rings. Her face pops up on my phone and I smile. I last saw her in person before moving in July but she's grown so much since. She may only be sixteen but Crystal will always be my baby sister.

"Oh, finally!" My sister says. "Dad was worried, you know."

I roll my eyes. "No, he wasn't." Though with my dad, it's possible. He has this panic mode that Mom called "Defcon Ultra," which is a pretty accurate representation. When we lost Mom, it got worse.

"Oh yeah," she says. "You didn't contact us at all last month."

"Because I was busy with midterms," I remind her.

My sister narrows her eyes at me. "Not that busy, Di."

Thankfully, Dad enters the frame before I can answer Crystal's question, and his brown eyes light up in relief. "*Mijita!*"

I laugh softly. "*Hola, papá.*"

"How are you? Passing your classes? Staying safe? No drugs or drinking?" Dad asks in Spanish. He stacks one question after the other like a rushed game of Jenga and I have to ask him to repeat. I grew up speaking Spanish because neither of my parents wanted Crystal and me to lose touch with our roots but it's still hard to keep up with him.

"Calm down, Dad." With how fast he's talking, you'd think there was a fire. I try to update him on my classes but he freaks out about my calculus class—hello? Scholarship kid over here—because of course he does. It's in his nature to be worried about me.

"Did you fix it?"

I nod, smiling about that ninety I received. "My grade is better than ever."

Crystal finally takes over the screen. "What's that smile for?"

Almost instantly, my smile disappears. "What smile?"

"Don't act coy with me, Di," she accuses. "You look like a lovesick puppy."

"Crystal, when have you ever known me to be lovesick?"

"Fair point." She taps a finger to her chin in thinking. "Oh, did I tell you about my driver's test? I passed!"

At the mention of driving, my heart drops slightly but I don't show it on my face. "That's great! On the first try?"

She smiles brightly as she nods. "It was so scary but I did it. My actual license doesn't come in for a few more weeks but I can finally go to the beach without Dad now."

"Hey," Dad calls. "I'm a fun chauffeur."

"I didn't say you weren't," she calls back.

"I'm proud of you, Crys," I tell her. My little sister got her driver's license before me. I really am proud of her but at the mention of driving, my heart starts pounding in my head. "Mom would be too."

Crystal's eyes soften at the mention of Mom. She was only nine when I got into that car accident. Only nine when we lost our mother that same night, so it hadn't affected her as it did me. She's lucky to still carry that optimism she was born with. A perfect balance to my type A pessimism that's terrified of stepping into a moving vehicle, no matter how hard I try to combat it these days.

Even when I prepare myself for the eventual worst, I always feel like I'm taking ten steps backward.

"Thanks, Di." Crystal's gratitude brings me back to the present and out of the deep and dark place of my thoughts. It's a bad route to go—the road where all my self-doubt and insecurities lie.

I finally feel the sun hit my face as Crystal continues to tell me more about her basketball season as well as her friends. I still can't believe that she's already a junior in high school. She's got a more prominent social life at that age than I did.

I hear the door open and turn to the back door. Huh, no one's outside. I swear I heard a creaking door. Shrugging, I turn back to my phone screen and, out of the corner of my eye, I spot it.

Or rather, him.

I swallow as quietly as I can because the sight in front of me is equally surprising. Carson Ryder, right outside his door. More specifically, a shirtless Carson with running shorts, a pair of worn-out sneakers, and ankle-high white socks.

Why are shirtless men my Achilles heel? Better yet—why can men just roll out of bed and look like that? With no fucking effort? It's highly unfair to the straight female gaze.

Almost instantly, the words I threw at his face on Wednesday come back to haunt my brain and I wince. Visibly.

"Diana!" Crystal shouts. Wow. With those lungs, she could wake up the entire street I'm on through the phone. She should have joined cheer instead.

"Sorry," I apologize, faking a yawn. "I'm still a little tired."

She furrows her brows. "You seemed fine earlier. Maybe you do need some sleep. It's what, six in the morning over there? Don't you have anything else to do? A party to host?"

I shake my head. "On a Sunday? No. No to all of that." Especially because I planned to finish off the cherry tarts sitting in my fridge while watching *Gilmore Girls*.

Crystal doesn't believe me and I can tell by the slight eyeroll. "I saw that!"

"Saw what?" She asks, fake innocence lacing her hazel-green eyes that are very similar to my own. Eyes we inherited from our mother. "I'm going to drink a cherry cola and leave you be. Good day, sister. And you better tell me what's getting you distracted."

My eyes instinctively move to Carson's front door, and he's not there.

"Or who." She wiggles her eyebrows before I roll *my* eyes and disconnect the call.

I lean against the outer wall of my house and let out a breath, closing my eyes. Though Mom's birthday has gotten easier, it's still hard to remember a day like this—a celebration of life for someone who's not alive. I've come to terms with a lot of things after Mom's death but the pain of losing her always lingers.

"You okay?"

Opening my eyes, I find Carson leaning on the wall, arms crossed over his ivory shoulders, accentuating the anchor tattoo on his bicep. For some reason, I always thought he was much more tan than he is. He's been living in California for as long as I have, if not way longer. Wouldn't he have tanned at least slightly?

I'm not complaining because he's always been handsome to me. That never changed from the day he threw a pie in my face.

"Diana?"

I blink. "Did you ask something?"

He nods slowly, blue eyes trained on me. "Yeah. Are you okay? You seem tired."

I rub an eye. "It's early. Why are *you* up?"

He jabs a thumb at the gate. "I'm going on a run. And I didn't mean physically tired."

Emotionally. Is it that obvious? "This early?" I ask.

He nods. "If daylight savings was still going on, it would have been earlier."

All alone?

Carson raises a brow. "Yeah. Why? Did you want to join me?" Dammit, I said that out loud. I feel like I could get distracted easily if I went on a run with him.

But running would always take my mind off everything. I loved being a part of the cross country and track teams in high school. That was probably one of my favorite things to do. And I haven't had time to go running because settling into college and work got in the way of any extra time I had.

Until today.

Should I stay at home and start my *Gilmore Girls* marathon early? Or do I go on a morning jog with a guy who has my heart racing? Well, as good as those cherry tarts sound, I need to clear my head now more than ever.

And running always helps.

I look down at my robe and fuzzy slippers before back up at Carson. "Give me a minute to change."

20

The Most Impulsive Thing I've Ever Done

Carson

Diana is both a silent and fast jogger.

The moment we started on the path around the streets of our neighborhoods, she started running like the devil was at her heels. If this is a light jog for her, then I've got my work cut out for me because I usually don't start this fast.

I've been waking up early to jog every Sunday for years. Alone, because none of my roommates particularly enjoy waking up at this hour. This is the first time someone has joined me on a run, even if said person is a couple of feet in front of me.

I quicken my pace to catch up to her; soon enough, we're jogging in silence. All of her dark hair—except her curtain bangs—is pulled up into a high ponytail and swishing back and forth.

"Starting strong, today?" I ask, desperate to break the silence for the first time. "You're running like hell is at your feet."

She scoffs, slowing down slightly. "This is a run, isn't it?"

"It's a jog," I say. "Not a race against your inner demons."

"What makes you think I have inner demons?" She challenges. This girl could be carrying the whole world on her shoulders and you wouldn't be able to notice just by the challenging gleam in her beautiful hazel-green eyes.

"Everyone has inner demons," I say shrugging. "Besides, you seemed a little beaten down after that phone call. Trouble in Miami?"

The sparkle in her eye is gone almost instantly. "Not trouble, exactly," she huffs as we reach an incline. "It's my mom's birthday."

98

Judging by the melancholy in her voice, that's not a great thing. "And you called your mom to wish her a happy birthday? That's all?"

"I didn't call my mom, Carson," she says. "Can we drop it?"

I decide not to prod her for more details and we run in silence for a little longer. Usually, I like the quiet. Today, however, the air between us is almost a little too thick. So much so that I could barely make a dent with the sharpest steak knife in the world.

We reach a cross-section near the campus village and wait for the signal to cross. I'm watching the streets, each car passing by when Diana finally speaks up.

"This is usually just not an easy day for me."

I turn to face her. She's not looking in my direction but merely watching each car pass like I was a moment ago. "Terrible relationship with your mom?"

"Far from it." She plays with the ends of her curtain bangs. "She was my best friend."

"Was?"

Diana nods. "She died seven years ago. I know that's a long time to be dead but I can't help but still miss her, you know?"

The light switches and Diana and I cross the street, resuming our jog. "Of course, it's not. She was your mom." I may not have lost anyone close to me in the past twenty years—and I'm thankful for that—so I can't know exactly what she's been through.

"Exactly." She quickens her pace.

"Do you even know what direction we're going?"

"Just following my gut," she calls back. Her gut, in question, is right in the village. More specifically, next to Trader Joe's. Grabbing a snack does sound appealing but I need to pause for a bit.

We make our way over to a small cluster of chairs. Since it's still early, the village is eerily quiet for a Sunday morning. Most of the tables are empty and it's just me and Diana. There are many seats at the table we choose but the moment we both sit down, it's right next to each other.

I try to hide the stupid grin about to stretch my face. "Does it hurt still?" I ask, motioning to her bare wrist.

She shakes her head. "Only a little, but not enough. I don't need it right now."

"Has it always been like this?" I mentally curse myself for asking a dumb question. *No, Ryder. Who the fuck could have been born with an injury like that?*

"No," she answers, not visibly noticing the stupidity of my question. "I broke my wrist in a car accident a few years back. Couldn't afford treatment at the time so it never healed properly."

My eyes widen. "Shit, I shouldn't have said anything."

Diana waves a hand to dismiss it. "Nah, you deserve to know some of the details since you helped. Seven years and this is the least amount of pain I've felt on my hand for an extended time so thanks." She sends me a small smile. "Again."

I'm about to respond before I remember something else she had told me. Holy fuck, I hope that what I'm thinking is wrong. "Seven years?"

She nods, getting up from her chair. "I can see the gears in your brain turning, Carson."

"You know what I was going to ask?"

"Yeah." She holds out her left hand and I grab it, standing myself up. Whether that yes is directed to the unasked question looming in the air or not, I'm not sure. "Same scenario. I nearly died that night but my mom did, because a drunk driver didn't know his right from his left on a Friday night."

Just like that, the last puzzle piece of Diana Blanco fit into place. To me, it explains a lot about her. Why she doesn't like rollercoasters or why she was about to pass out from sitting in Jake's car. It wasn't motion sickness—and I know better than anyone else what that looks like—it was a panic attack.

"What are you thinking?" She asks, breaking me out of my thoughts. And a good thing she did because I don't want to imagine Diana in that situation again.

I think that I might get sick if I ever think about it again.

I shake my head. "Nothing you'd find interesting, I assure you."

"You can still talk about it," she insists. "I won't judge you."

"Not right now." I glance over at the streets, the area much busier than it had been when we first arrived. "Race you back home?"

The twinkle in her eyes appears at the mention of a challenge. "What does the winner get?"

"I'll decide when we get there," I say.

She scoffs. "What makes you think you're going to win?"

"Easy." I lean closer to her. Our foreheads could be touching but I manage to restrain myself. Her cheeks turn red and I can sense her heavy breathing and we haven't even started running. Just being this close has my heart beating in my ears. She must be feeling this too, right?

I could close the distance right here and now. It's tempting but I manage to resist. "Because I don't lose." I dash off in the direction of home with Diana shouting not far behind.

"What the fuck? That wasn't fair, man!"

I start to laugh as I pass the restaurants and parking lots. I finally reach the crosswalk before Diana catches up and she doesn't even seem out of breath. I know I am and it has nothing to do with running.

"That was cheating!" She complains right beside me.

"I didn't say start."

"Well, distracting me like that still counts," she states. "Besides, actually kissing me would have been much more effective."

The statement catches me off-guard and I nearly trip over a crack in the sidewalk, allowing Diana to move farther ahead and I try my best to catch up. Thankfully, we're stopped and I manage to catch up with her.

"I've got one." I press my hand to my knees, catching my breath for a minute. "The winner gets to ask the loser any question they want."

"That's it?" She furrows her brows. "One question?"

"One question. About anything."

That definitely piques her interest. "Anything? Even…"

I nod. "Yup."

"Deal."

We're then given the signal to cross and we run like hell. It takes us a while to even reach the house but by the time we do, Emma is sitting out by the lawn chairs, reading a book with a cover that would make my sister blush.

She looks up at us running and her eyes widen as she scrambles off the chair. Diana and I both reach for the chair. Our hands touch the chair at the same time, my left hand next to hers.

"What did I just witness?" She mumbles to herself.

"Emma!" Diana grabs her hand and brings her closer to the chair. "Who do you think won? We were racing."

"Uh..." Emma glances between the two of us. Both sweaty and a little out of breath. "I wasn't paying attention. Please, if this is a fight, then don't get me involved. Just kiss and makeup or something. I'm calling a tie."

She then grabs her book that she dropped and heads back inside Diana's house, the door shut behind her.

I stare at the door. "Well, she was—"

"Yeah," she agrees. "But we surprised her and she hates surprises."

I nod, totally understanding what she just said—even though I do not. "So, it looks like I won."

"No way! I got here first. See?" We look back down at the arms of the chair. Both of our hands are touching the same arm but—something I didn't notice at first glance—the tip of her finger sits atop my knuckle.

"How do you explain that, then?" I gesture to the placement of our hands.

"You moved my finger."

"Diana," I sigh. "I moved nothing. You lost by a finger. Though I must admit, you were a tough competitor. Did you do track or something?"

She nods. "And cross country all four years of high school." Wiping the sweat on her forehead with the back of her hand, she closes her eyes and she's not breathing as heavily. "Is that your one question?"

"Nope. I'd do better than that."

"Well, ask away," she says, plopping herself down on the chair. "I might as well be an open book."

I allow myself to ponder that question. Honestly, I should have let Diana ask me a question instead because I've learned a lot more about her than she has of me.

But the tiny part of my brain wants to be selfish and ask more because I *want* to know more.

"Coming from someone who's never been through something like that," I begin with. "Was it that terrifying?"

"Going deep aren't you?" She chuckles before getting serious. "Without going into much detail, yes. A near-death experience could change someone. I was terrified of it happening again. So I avoided drinking, parties—anything that could lead to a similar occurrence. Even motor vehicles when I had the chance."

"No driving?"

She gives me a look. "That was two questions."

"I'm just saying. You live in California now, a state that practically requires driving from one place to another. Not once have you thought about learning how?"

Diana opens her mouth slightly before closing it. This is the first time I've ever seen her hesitate on anything. "Well, I am trying."

I frown slightly. "Trying?"

"I got my learner's permit back in July but with everything going on and school being at walking distance, I just never had to chance to ask Ronnie to teach me." She leans a little closer and lowers her voice. "Plus, I've been scared to ask."

"Scared?" I question. "The Diana I know is fearless."

"Well," she says, shrugging. "I've been scared my entire life."

Scared my entire life. Holy shit, that's sad. I can't imagine the slightest picture of what Diana went through but I want to so badly tell her that she's a survivor. She shouldn't let one moment dictate how she lives her life moving forward.

Maybe I can show her. An idea forms in my head and I choose to act on it.

"What's that look?" Diana asks wearily.

I shake my head. "Not important. Do you have anything planned for today?"

She shakes her head.

I stand up from my chair. "Meet me back out here with your purse in an hour, okay?"

"Am I allowed to ask questions?"

Chuckling, I ask, "Do you trust me?"

"Do you really want me to answer that question?"

"Just trust me," I assure her before heading towards my front door and entering my house.

"You better not steal my stuff!" She shouts before I close the door behind me.

Trust me, if anyone's gonna be stealing anything, it's her. She already stole my heart anyway.

21

Just Feeling It
Diana

I'm sure I set the record for the fastest time ever. The speed at which I got ready for the day could rival Hermes—and that messenger god isn't known for being slow. I, however, take an obscene amount of time to just style my hair.

Now I stand outside in the clearing between our houses, waiting for Carson. Purse in hand, sunglasses perched on the bridge of my smaller-than-average nose, light cream-colored sweater, and jeans that hang slightly low on my hips. It's still chilly outside but with the sun shining bright on us, you wouldn't notice.

After another minute passes, Carson's front door opens and he steps out. Once again, the son of a bitch looks handsome without even trying. Coiffed brown hair and a washed-out jean jacket layered atop a white hoodie with the words, "Bored of South-Sea." Jesus, I know he's not a skater but he can pull that look off so effortlessly. Especially with that smile.

If my insides weren't already swarming with every butterfly imaginable, they would be now.

Carson holds up a set of keys and shakes them. "You ready?"

My eyes widen. "We're driving?"

"We can't get there walking," he explains. "Highways exist."

Looks like I'm already a dead girl walking.

"This better be worth it," I mutter as I follow him out to where Jake's car is parked. I take over the passenger's side while Carson makes himself comfortable behind the wheel before reaching into his pocket and pulling out a bottle of—

"Dramamine?" I blurt out. "Why did you bring Dramamine?" I don't feel any motion sickness when I'm in a moving vehicle. Just panic.

He opens the bottle and swallows one pill before starting the engine. "It's mainly for me but you can have some if you need it."

"You get car sick?"

"Sadly." He moves the gearshift and the car starts moving backward, startling me. On instinct, I grab onto the handlebar with my right hand, not caring that I might regret it eventually.

"You're not the only one who has a weakness with motor vehicles," he tells me. "It's not as bad when I'm behind the wheel but last time Jake drove with me in the car…" He visibly winces. "Let's just say it wasn't pretty. I've been the designated driver ever since."

"And he's okay with that?"

He shrugs. "If it means he gets control of the aux, then I don't think he cares." We finally stop at a red light before he turns to face me. "Speaking of, did you want to play any songs?"

"I'm not picky," I answer. "You decide."

Carson shakes his head. "Nah, it's the rule. The passenger picks the music."

"I should not be in charge of the music." Because I never know what to pick. I don't freeze up on the spot but when it comes to music, my brain draws so many blanks that it would take a truck filled with cement to close them. "Please, Carson. Just pick something. I'm truly okay with whatever you choose."

He tilts his head for a second before reaching for his phone and tapping on it. Probably to pick a song or playlist. It has me thinking: what genre of music does Carson listen to? Alt-rock? Hip-hop? Hell, I wouldn't even be surprised if Taylor Swift starts playing.

But when I hear "Someone New" by Hozier spill through the car speakers, I'm utterly taken by surprise. God, I never thought that a guy could get hotter because of his taste in music but a guy who listens to Hozier? That alone may or may not have turned me on.

Just slightly.

3 . 1 4 1 5 9 2 6 5 3 5 9

Carson pulls into a parking lot and turns off the engine. Huh? Why did he stop? "Are we already there?" I ask him.

"No, we're only halfway," he tells me, unbuckling his seatbelt and opening the car door. "You're going to take us the rest of the way."

My jaw drops at his announcement. "I...but...what??"

"That's my plan." He closes his door and quickly rounds the car to open my door. "You said you never got a hands-on lesson, so I'm going to give you one."

Forget the dropping jaw—I'm frozen in my seat. "But, what about your motion sickness? I could be so bad that we'd have to pull over and—"

"Why do you think I brought the Dramamine?" He offers his hand and I slowly take it, feeling the warmth of his grasp. "Besides, you won't be the worst driver with me teaching you.

"But—"

"You never know unless you try."

I take a deep breath and round the car over to the dreaded driver's side. Never in my life have I been so complacent until this very moment. With each step I take, I'm closer to my biggest fear—okay, second-biggest fear.

"Diana." Carson's voice breaks through my panic but I can't face him. My limbs are stuck. I'm not moving a muscle. *Why are you doing this, Carson?*

"We're gonna die!" I say.

"No, we won't," he assures me in a calm tone. How the fuck is he not freaking out? "I will instruct you on what to do. The engine's also off. Turn it on first and *then* you can start panicking."

"This is not the time for sarcasm, Carson!"

"Diana, listen. I know you're terrified. But here's the situation: you're the one in control, here. You're the one who decides how fast the car moves, which way to turn, and how fast to break. I'll give you directions on where to go but the road ahead is yours. You can't let that fear control your life anymore." I feel his hand touch my bare knee—my jeans are ripped—and I feel my chest moving. Okay, at least I'm breathing.

My head finally turns to him and his blue eyes meet mine, not starting away for a nanosecond.

"Grab life by the steering wheel and get moving." A determined smile caresses his face. He trusts me to get us to whatever location he had in mind.

All I need is to trust myself. So I press the red button, start the engine, and slowly ease my foot onto the gas pedal. Carson instructs me on which direction to turn so I don't hit anything because if Jake found out, he'd murder us—Carson's words, not mine.

I leave the parking lot and it's mostly smooth driving from here. Which means we're stuck in traffic the closer we get to Marbella Beach, a beach town just off the Pacific Coast Highway. Especially because we're taking the long route that avoids the freeway entrances.

Each minute that passes, I can't help but think of how considerate this is. If I'm being honest, I would have chickened out at the last minute so the surprise—although terrifying—is definitely appreciated.

While we're stuck at another red light, the music stops. I guess Carson forgot to queue another one. Might as well rip the band-aid off and say something. "About the whole 'selfish' thing last week—"

He cuts me off. "If you're about to apologize, Diana, then don't."

"But it was a little rude of me."

"You weren't wrong," he says. "It just took someone else aside of me to confirm it." He leans back on the seat, practically sinking into it.

I should probably mention that throughout this whole ordeal, his hand never leaves my knee. He kept it there when we left the parking lot and now? That same left hand holds onto it tighter as if my bare knee is an anchor.

"If there's something you should know about me, it's that I would do anything to get people to like me. If they need a hand, I'd give them my whole arm. If your life was built on fear, then mine is built on destroying a person's hatred towards me. Doing absolutely anything to help but never expect anything in return because that would make me 'greedy.'" He adds air quotes. "I can rant about that all I want but we don't have enough hours in the day for me to do so."

The light turns green and I slowly press the gas pedal with my right foot, quickly glancing over to him. "In short, you're a people pleaser?"

He nods. "I try to avoid conflict if it means things would be easier."

"Must have made you popular," I muse.

"It definitely made me tired."

"Then why don't you stop?" I ask, to which he scoffs.

"Oh, *Just Diana*. If only it were that easy."

"But it is." We approach another red light almost immediately. With that, I place all of my attention to him. "You can't please everyone, Carson. There will always be disagreements around you. I know you try your best to settle those disputes but if you don't take the time to figure out what you want—" I jab a finger at his chest with my free hand—"then you'll end up being the one who suffers the most. At some point, you'll have to do something for *yourself*. Not for others."

Carson's expression is unreadable. I can't tell what he's thinking. Could he be annoyed with what I just said? Is he still processing it? I don't know.

But when he exhales, I realize that he might have needed to hear those words.

"I'm trying but it's hard."

My hand reaches his shoulder, rubbing it. "No one said it was easy."

The light finally turns green and Carson points to the road. "Turn left here," he instructs me.

After what feels like an eternity, he finally directs me to a parking space near the downtown area and a town called Marbella Beach. I turn on the engine and just like that, I feel a weight lift off my shoulders and Carson's hand finally lifts from my knee.

"I just drove to Marbella Beach," I mutter to myself. Holy shit, I did it! And made it in one piece.

"See?" He exits the car and just as I'm about to exit, Carson rounds the car and opens the door for me, holding out his hand. "I knew you could do it. We're alive, I don't feel too sick, and you faced your fear."

Probably one of my biggest accomplishments yet. I grab his hand and close the door behind me. We make our way toward the beach, talking about the sights we saw during the drive over. How the giant spider on some random guy's bald head terrified me.

We're almost at the pier when someone's beach ball splashes on the sand in front of us and I get sand inside my shoes. I remove my shoes and socks and just continue walking barefoot.

"Thanks again," I tell Carson. "Today might just be a day to remember."

"The day you saw that spider?" He gives me a wry smile, and I laugh. We drove by a bald guy with a spider on his head. It was a little scary.

"Oh definitely," I agree, getting a laugh out of him. "You know what would be even better?"

He raises a brow, clearly curious at what I have to say. "What would?"

I raise my chin slightly. "A rematch for that race."

The other brow flies up. "You sure you want to lose again?"

"What makes you think I'll lose again?" I ask. Running in the sand is my forte. I mean, hello? Miami native here? That was basically my entire childhood. "I could easily whip your ass."

"Then prove it," he challenges, pointing to the stairs that lead up to the pier. "Last person who reaches the bottom of that staircase has to pay for lunch."

"Bring it on." I quickly slip my shoes back on and take off laughing without another care.

"I didn't say start!" He calls out, jogging after me.

"We'll call it even!" I shout back. Running in dry sand is not easy, I tell you. So it doesn't take very long for Carson to catch up to me.

We're neck in neck—or head and neck, since the guy is six feet tall, give or take an inch—and just as I pass a vendor, I trip on a small hill of sand and fall stomach-down onto it.

"Diana!"

I find myself laughing as I pull myself up to a sitting position because I can't remember the last time I felt so... light. Without a care in the world. When was the last time I felt that way?

"I'm okay," I assure him in between laughs. "It doesn't hurt."

He bends down to my level. "Your wrist isn't hurting?"

Shaking my head, I reach for his knee and snake my hand around to the back of his ankle. "I am just fine." With one motion and two hands, I reach for his foot and trip him. Carson falls on his back with a light thump—dry sand doesn't hurt as much as wet sand, luckily.

"Warn a guy, don't you," he jokes.

I move so that I'm lying myself next to him, turning on my side so I face him. I couldn't care if I got sand in my hair. "Where's the fun in that?"

He turns onto his side so he faces me, and our faces are merely inches from each other. "You are something else when the whole world isn't on your shoulders."

And the butterflies are back. My face is already splitting in half with how big my smile is. "Is that a good thing?" I ask, my breathing getting heavier with each second.

Maybe I'm imaging this but Carson moves much closer. In fact, so close that our noses are almost touching. Is it really going to happen? Please let this be real because I will be pissed if a beach ball interrupts this.

If this isn't happening, send me a sign.

A beat passes, and nothing happens. Well, nothing except for the swift movement where he closes the distance between us and I freeze. Wait, I wanted this to happen. Why am I not doing anything?

Before I can reciprocate, he pulls back. "I'm sorry. I didn't read that correctly, did—"

I bring my hand to the back of his neck and pull his soft lips to mine, doing what I should have done when he made the first move. Gosh, I've been wanting to do that since the maze on my birthday.

Thankfully, he kisses me back, with much more confidence and I find myself melting into it. His arm wraps around my waist, pulling me right to his chest and I melt into his touch, wishing that he doesn't let go.

I'm staying in the moment. Not letting another fear get in the way of this because I know one thing: he wanted this too.

So why should I try to talk myself out of it?

22

Together

Carson

My memory can be spacious, but that kiss has taken over my entire brain.

It only happened about an hour ago and I still wish that stupid beach ball didn't spray sand all over us. I couldn't even find it in me to care that I got sand all over my jacket.

But the moment was ruined. That didn't stop my brain from spinning in circles at the events.

I kissed Diana Blanco.

I fucking kissed her and she kissed me back!

She wanted to kiss me. This almost feels like a high school crush even though we're both twenty-year-olds in our third year of university. But the giddiness of kissing the girl I've fallen for still feels the same. Except, while my teenage self was filled with nothing but nerves, this time around I feel a sort of coziness.

We're now sitting at a bench on the pier, looking over the very same beach. I don't want to break the silence between us, but we've literally said nothing else since that happened.

All we did was grab sodas—I'm halfway through a water bottle while she's slowly sipping a cherry Coke, to no one's surprise—and place ourselves on this bench.

One minute we were talking about our biggest secrets and the next...nothing but the sound of silence fills the space between us.

A silence that one of us has to break. And it might just be me even if it's with something stupid.

"What do we do now?" Like this. Yeah, that's a question I just asked. *Way to fucking go, Ryder.* My nerves are bouncing inside my head like a crazy table tennis ball because I am truly speechless.

We both are.

"It's only one, right? We've still got time," she responds, her gaze still aimed at the beautiful view in front of us. Though my eyes only focus on her.

"That's not what I'm talking about, Diana."

She sighs, shifting herself so that her entire body faces me. Her hair still has some bits of sand and I reach my hand out to dust it all off. Diana doesn't say anything for a while but once I move my hand away from her hair, she speaks.

"Maybe we should just start walking," she suggests before standing up from the bench. Wow, she's desperate to avoid this topic, isn't she?

"What?"

Oh shit, I must have been staring.

"I've never been here, you know," she continues. "Might as well see what this pier has to offer."

"Okay." I stand up from the bench and follow her.

We pass a couple of the restaurants before finally reaching the farther end of the pier, away from the screaming kids on the rollercoaster and wannabe rappers. Diana leans forward on the railing, soda still in hand, twirling the top of the bottle between her fingers.

"I don't know." Her eyes are trained on the top half of the bottle she's fiddling with. "I'm not exactly sure, to be honest. It's a little scary."

"Scary?" I arch a brow.

"Not knowing what to do next," she clarifies. "I mean, I went from calling you an overgrown child, which I'm sorry about, by the way, to now and—"

"Let me guess," I interrupt, dismissing the small apology. "It's terrifying?"

She nods and her hazel eyes finally stare into me. "Very. It's easy when I can just figure this all out on my but I can't now."

Diana takes a breath to continue but I hold my hand up. "Sorry, but can I stop you right there, again?"

"Yeah."

"All on your own? That seems exhausting," I remark.

She shrugs helplessly. "I've managed to do a lot on my own. It's not that hard."

"But you don't have to. You should never feel that you have to do everything on your own, no matter what. If you want to, that's a whole different scenario."

"I can take care of myself, you know," she argues.

"There's no doubt about that," I agree. "But there's a lot of people in your corner who would do anything to help you. *Including* me."

Her eyes widen slightly.

"Do you know the one thing I admired about you most?" I ask her. "That you wouldn't visibly judge me and it made telling you stuff a lot easier than it would with someone like Jake. Or even my sister." And those two have known me longer than Diana. I don't tell either of them about how it feels to not do something for myself.

But I told Diana.

"But I'm—"

"Not great with talking?" I had a hunch when she kept herself silent around me after the pie incident. "I don't want you to feel scared to talk to me. If that's the case, then I'm not doing my job of being a somewhat decent person."

"I'm not," she tells me. "I'm just worried this"—she motions her hand between us—"could be too fast."

"Then we'll go slow." I take her free hand in my own, holding it lightly since it's her right hand that I know still flares up. "We talk about it, and we figure it out. I want to figure this all out, too, but I want to do it with you."

She stops twirling the bottle with her left hand but keeps a firm grasp on it.

"I want to do it with you too," she says softly. I could kiss her again right now but I hold myself back. "But I'm scared."

"Then we'll be scared together." I smile softly at her, hopefully assuring her that she's not alone. "Besides, if we can get through calculus, then I think we can survive anything." I wink and a small laugh escapes her lips.

"Yeah, nothing was tougher than optimization," she groans.

"We'll have to do it all over again for the final," I remind her, to which she shakes her head vehemently.

"Fuck. That."

I shake my head and we both start laughing.

"Could it really be that easy?"

"Talking? Simple. Just like this." I let go of her hand, stepping closer to her. Placing one hand on her cheek, I inch myself closer to her. "Can I kiss you?"

Her breath tickles my nose and she nods. I close the distance between us and she pulls me closer with the straps of my sweatshirt until there's just about no space left between us.

It doesn't feel fast to me. If anything, it feels fucking right. There will be times when we don't agree on random shit but something tells me that, regardless of what happens, we'll be alright.

Besides, this is only the beginning.

Hard to believe that this all started with a pie to the face, right?

Epilogue - Full Circle Moments
Diana

December

"You sure he's not gonna see me here?" I ask Jake before stepping inside the closet, along with Lucia and Carly.

"Don't worry," he assures me. "It's dark in there and he won't see you girls."

After finishing my finals this morning, a lightbulb lit up in my head and I had to relay it to Jake—because it's a surprise for Carson. Sure, it requires me to hide in my boyfriend's bedroom closet, but it will be so worth it.

Everyone else has left for the holidays except for us—me, Jake, Lucia, Carly, and Carson—so I planned this little hurrah to celebrate the end of the winter term. And for the dreaded calculus finally ending.

Thank the fucking gods that Scott's useless lectures are over. Though I have to give him credit—if it wasn't for them, I wouldn't have spent all that time with Carson. We still kept up with those sessions—though he started calling them study dates instead.

"Thanks, anyway."

"So I bring him here and you will attack him with the pie?"

I nod.

"What a full circle moment," he mutters, mostly to himself.

"Yeah," Lucia agrees from the other side of the closet. "Nothing says romance like exacting revenge."

"I'm confused," Carly says, holding the pie with both hands. "What revenge?"

Jake and Lucia then explain to Carly the day Carson and I met and she chuckles in response. "That does not sound like Carson. I'm supposed to be the troubled twin."

"Not troubled enough," Jake mutters. Carly reaches over me to punch Jake's arm with her free hand. "You know what? I'm going to leave you girls here and not earn any more bruises from Rocky Balboa here."

Jake slides the closet door closed and the three of us sit alone in the dark. At least, until Lucia speaks up.

"Uh, Carly? Your arm is tangled in my braids."

"Sorry! I'm trying not to get meringue all over them."

I pull out my phone from my back pocket and turn on the flashlight, allowing the girls to see better. One of Lucia's braids is wrapped partially around Carly's elbow and the two girls untangle it the best they can. I jump in to help but I'm not sure that made the process any faster.

I grab the pie from Carly's hand with my left hand and try to balance it with one hand while waiting for Carson to take the bait.

Almost instantly, I hear shuffling from the other side of the door and I shush Carly and Lucia.

"Jake, why did you leave Bailey's gift in my room?" Carson took the bait.

"Because it was easier to hide in your closet! You have all those sweat-shirts."

"When was the last time you saw my closet? Because I haven't seen half of those things in the past month."

My cheeks heat up, knowing damn well that half of his hoodies have surprisingly ended up in my room. They're *super* comfortable, okay? Especially the red one I'm wearing.

"Fine," Carson huffs as he slides the closet door open. I don't give him enough time to react before...

Splat!

The pretty face is now covered in pie. *Yes, I finally got him!* I jump and laugh in joy and celebrate, while Carly's head pops out of the closet, taking in the scene. She joins me in my laughter and Lucia follows shortly after.

Carson wipes the filling from his eyes and gives me a questioning look. It's hard to take someone covered in pie from the neck up seriously. I'm holding back giggles to the best of my ability but—as handsome as he is—my boyfriend looks so fucking goofy with lemon meringue pie all over his face.

I'm still not used to calling him my boyfriend, by the way. I went from calling him an overgrown child back in July to calling him my boyfriend.

"I thought you were Jake right there," I say. He can't even get mad at me for this.

Thankfully, he doesn't. Instead, he just shakes his head while licking some of the meringue from his mouth. My eyes dart to his mouth quickly before moving back up to his eyes. *Keep your composure, D.*

He chuckles. "Oh, I see how it is, D."

"How what is?" I ask innocently.

"You can't fool me."

I shake my head. "I'm not fooling anyone."

"Just gloating about your revenge."

"What does gloating look like?" I question with my chin raised.

That smirk I've come to know so well appears. "Why don't you step closer and find out?"

"Okay," Lucia's voice interjects. "I'm going to step outside right now because I refuse to get any pie filling on me with God knows what you'll do next."

"Same," Carly agrees, following Lucia out of the bedroom. Jake is the last one to leave. While walking out, he mutters: "I can't look at pie the same way since *that* movie," but I don't ask what he's talking about.

I don't care, either because now it's just me and Carson. Alone. In his room.

"How long have you wanted to do that?" He asks.

I grin mischievously. "Since three hours ago."

He raises a brow, not completely believing me.

I sigh. "Okay, since the day you threw that pie at me."

"I regret nothing," he hums, snaking one arm around my waist. "I got to meet you, didn't I?"

"Yep," I answer. He leans closer and just as my eyes flutter shut, waiting for our lips to press against each other, something sticky grazes my cheeks. My hands rise to my face and feel the pie filling. I narrow my eyes at Carson. "Oh, it's on."

I reach for the pie tin on the floor and grab a handful of pie before smearing it over his face. Some of the goop falls onto the floor, while the rest lies right on top of his shoes.

He retaliates by attempting the same, but I manage to dodge it by ducking under his arm as he attempts to reach for me a second time. Unfortunately, it lands on my hair and I fall onto his bed, with him on top of me, laughing.

With that, Carson brings his hand behind my head and pulls me in for a kiss. Just a peck at first before I place my hand around the back of his and pull him closer, deepening the kiss. I smile against his lips. Even if we weren't just flinging pie filling at each other, Carson would still taste sweet.

"You know, I'm going to get you back for that," he murmurs against my lips, causing me to giggle.

I pull away, breaking the kiss. "Nah, you love me too much to tip the scales again," I joke.

He sighs. "Yeah, you're right." His fingers play with my curtain bangs. "I can just call it payback for all my missing sweatshirts." Carson eyes the one I'm wearing and smirks.

"I think we should just stick to the pies and call it even." I pat his chest before maneuvering myself around Carson to stand up. I reach for the ceiling, stretching my arms out. "Besides, you promised me another driving lesson."

Since Marbella Beach, Carson's made it his mission to teach me how to drive until I feel comfortable enough to take the test. It might be a while until I'm ready but I'm one step closer because of him.

Mom would love that I'm doing this. And she would have loved Carson as much as I do.

"But I also want to spend a few more minutes with my girlfriend," he insists, taking my hand and pulling me back into his embrace. "While we still have all this space."

I giggle, resting my head onto his chest. "We'll still have time later."

"But we can spare a few minutes before."

I lift my head slightly to meet his eyes—those pale blues that I've familiarized myself with and look forward to seeing everyday because I just know that I'm getting stronger and more confident in myself. And Carson Jameson Ryder will be in my corner.

Granted, I'm a girl who can stand her ground but I couldn't face a lot of obstacles head-on for years. It helps to surround myself with people who believe in me everyday.

"Alright," I relent. "Maybe a few minutes." Smiling, I press my lips to his for only a moment before quickly pulling away, trying to look as serious as I can in the moment. "But then you're teaching me."

Carson smirks. "Yes, ma'am."

Loved this and want to see more of Carson Ryder? Stay tuned for book 2 in the Ryder Twins duet, Carly's story!

Acknowledgements

Okay, if you were to tell me two years ago that I would be publishing this story, about this SPECIFIC pairing, I would have laughed in your face. This is just crazy to me. I still can't believe it, even as I'm typing this.

There's a lot of people I want to thank for making this possible. So let's get started.

Now, firstly, I want to thank my beta readers. You seriously are amazing and I appreciate your patience with me. Adelaide, Esther, Summer, Brooke, Reggie. Thank you girls!

Now, to Reggie, who deserves a separate paragraph. I love you so much for staying up late with me and helping me brainstorm the most hilarious things, as well as the cutest moments. This book wouldn't have been possible without you, and your talent with graphic design and art.

Oh, and your unhinged quotes that have ended up in this book.

To my ARC readers, who volunteered their time to read a novella from a debut author and post a review.

My roommates, who were so supportive from the first day we moved in together. It warms my heart to have people close by who support me.

And lastly, to you. The reader. I cannot thank you enough for taking a chance on a small, extremely new author like me. Here's to many more cute, funny, and heart-warming love stories.

For now and forever,
Daya James.

About the author

Daya James is an indie romance author born and raised in Southern California. She is a hopeless romantic obsessed with playlists and enjoys hearing back from those who feel the same about her love of romance and happily ever afters.

When not reading or writing about happily ever afters and boys that have topped her already high-enough standards, DJ inches closer and closer to earning her bachelor's degree.

She also can't stop singing or dancing. Really, she can't.

Also by Daya James

Ryder Twins Duet

The PI(E) Truce (Diana and Carson) – Out Now!
The Film Crew (Carly and Crew) – Coming soon!

More books to come soon!